Red Heaven

Nina Clotemans

Contents

I. Some Exploring In The Future

~ Present 2018

It was a serene afternoon in the town of Rangarh. The market place was bustling with vendors selling their goods and the sweetmeat sellers were busy cradling the golden - orange jalebis in their huge oil pots with an equally large ladles. Tourists were busy capturing the marvels of this town.

"Yes,yes come right here. Now this beauty you're seeing is the 296 years old fort of Rangarh. It was built in the year 1722 by the late Maharaj Aryaman Verma I. This fort has a lot of rich history and valour apart from all the wars the kings and the princes of this fort had fought as history sometimes forgets about a story revolving around the Princess of this colourful town ."

A voice echoed from the streets by a female tour guide with doe - eyed brown eyes, dark long hair and olive skin who seemed to be in her early twenties , pushed through the streets followed by a group of tourists both foreign and native that consisted totally of ten people, while pointing towards a part of the fort wall high atop a small hill in the centre of the town.

The fort wall was indeed a magnificent work of art as it was made of ochre sandstone and hints of blue and turquoise paintings on the exterior that hasn't faded even after 296 years.

" The name of this town ,Rangarh , was actually inspired from this fort and it's architecture . Rang means colour in Hindi and Garh means fort. This town was actually colourful in the previous era and the Hindu festival Holi was a big deal here because well.....Holi was the festival of colours. But everything changed when the British finally annexed the kingdom in 1862 and the people here forgot about their culture. Now the present generation are trying to bring back the lost glory of Rangarh," the tour guide explained with a sigh in the end.

The tourists were captured at the marvel of the fort wall and the surrounding ethereal beauty of the town.

" This architecture is just a masterpiece! And the colours contrast greatly along with it", a middle -aged foreign tourist man exclaimed with joy.

" Why yes sir ! The blueprint of this fort was exclusively designed by Maharaj Aryaman Verma I himself! He was a great lover of art and culture," the tour guide beamed.

" You're so lucky to live in this beautiful town! I would give anything to escape this city life of Delhi", a mother of a toddler girl voiced her opinion and wiped her sweaty forehead with the back of her hand.

" Can't say lucky but blessed, yes. Even though this place is simple it's elegant at the finest", the tour guide smiled at the lady and continued guiding the visitors throughout the town.

She veered them through the entrance of the fort after a tiresome climb from the hill steps. After they collected their tickets, she took the tourists throughout the fort, explaining each intricate details about the fort and it's palaces.

" The reason this fort was situated on top of a rocky hill was to protect it from invaders and enemies from capturing the kingdom and inflicting harm on the Royal family. Even though it was a small and simple kingdom, it was the strongest. The Verma family of Rangarh reigned for a 139 years without losing to anyone expect the British East India Company due to their high fortified kingdom and defences. The Mughals were a huge treat during the those times in Uttar Pradesh but Rangarh managed to keep a low profile and the terrain at that time was difficult to venture in."

" The British too had a hard time in conquering Rangarh, they tried for 5 years and finally won. The Rangarh soldiers were battle hardened people who would never go down without a fight, that's why their patron goddess is Durga, the Hindu goddess of protection, strength, motherhood, destruction and wars. Saraswathi was worshipped for her domain in arts, culture, music and knowledge. Both these goddess were important in Rangarh and still do till this date."

The tour guide recited the entire history in one breath. The foreign tourists were in awe of the story behind the simple town of Rangarh while the Indian visitors were shocked at the fact that was hidden from them for a long time.

They all entered into a part of the fort which was decorated extensively with a huge throne sitting in the midst of the room along with another one beside it, except that it was smaller than the other. Both the thrones were made of gold and were decorated with precious stones such as emeralds, rubies and sapphires.

Paintings and intensive traditional carvings adorned the room along with plush carpets.

" This is the Royal Durbar or the Royal courtroom of the late Vermas and the throne belongs to the Kings of the dynasty. There used to be a Prince's and Princess's throne but their origins are unknown. The hearings of the locals or other important matters with the King would take place in the Durbar", the tour guide yapped away to the tourists excitedly, clearly showing that she was proud of her town's history.

"You said something about the Princess earlier....What happened"? A teenage Indian girl asked from the crowd.

Before the tour guide could reply a man cut her off by saying, " Oh beta, the Princess is no big deal! We don't talk about her here.She was just a traitor to her own kingdom and her countrymen. That's why even our own townspeople don't remember much about her. All that is known in history was that she was that she turned her back against her own country and sided with the British for her own safety and greed , but when she didn't get the power that she desired, she turned on the Britishers too."

The tour guide was aghast at the man's accusation and tried to intervene, " that's not true Chacha! What you heard was wrong. The Princess never turned her back on anyone, it's just lies!

" Oh really Raina?Everyone in this town knows that Princess Sagarika was a complete and utter disgrace."

The man turned to the group of tourists who were listening to the heated conversation intently, and continued his accusation, " The Princess wanted the throne all for herself and desired power, that's why she became a spy for the British when they promised to make her the Queen of Rangarh. She wanted to overthrow her own brother, Maharaj Neelsingh Verma II, the last King of Rangarh, by giving him slow poison that deteriorated his health. When the King found out that his sister was plotting behind his back, he banished her from the Kingdom all together. You can go ask this to anyone in this town and they will all say the same as this is the truth."

The visitors believed the man which made the tour guide, Raina, upset. She had no power to tell them that this was all wrong because of the fact that she had no proof of it. After all, the talk about the Princess was a taboo.

People avoided talking about her story. They would frown with an offended expression when asked about the last Princess of Rangarh. Nothing much was known about her and the townspeople didn't care about her history.

When the sun went down in Rangarh and the fort had to close it's gates for the day, Raina returned back to her family Hotel in one of the streets of Rangarh along with some of the tourists who stayed there.

After having dinner she went to the library in the hotel to read some books. When scrounging through the shelves a book fell near her with a loud thud. Raina bent down to pick it up where the book lied. It looked quite odd that Raina was sure it was a journal of some sort but never has she seen this in her library.

She thought that it might be a new addition to the library that one of her family members brought in, but what perplexed her was that it was too old to be new as leather bits were tearing up at the front and back of the cover. The book was bind close with a ratty leather string.

Raina removed the leather string and opened the book to find pages that yellowed in time, as she guessed it indeed was a journal due to writings in the pages with ink. The writings were in English but the handwriting was too swirly for the normal cursive.

" Whoever owned this journal sure did have a beautiful handwriting. Wish mine was like that," Raina murmured while flipping through the pages.

She wasn't the one to pry into other people's diaries but this one had a mysterious and vintage aura around it that Raina just couldn't help herself but steal the old diary and hide it in her jacket.

On reaching her room on top of the hotel where there was a small apartment for her family members, Raina shut door to her room and hopped on the bed flipping to the first entry in the diary.

April 16, 1848

I've reached India as the Resident officer for Rangarh by the orders of the East India Company, taking up after my father Colonel Richard Smith. I've been trained my entire life for this, serving my country just like all of my family did.

After a long sail in the HMS Crown Jewel I finally made it to India at a cost of losing thirty crew members in a horrible plague. By the God's Grace, I did not contract any of that disastrous plague.

As the first task of being the Resident officer of Rangarh I'm supposed to collect taxes for the Company and familiarise with the Royal family.

I have no idea why on earth I've been put up with this desolate Indian kingdom . I don't want anything to do with these Indians that are under our control but I must continue to hold up our family's honour and name.

The Crown's sole reason to dispatch the 7th Queen's own hussars from the British Army was to reinforce the East India Company's armies and to maintain control in Rangarh.

The General told me to march into the Palace of Rangarh to collect the tributes from there and pay a visit to the Royal family. Especially the King. I know the main motive is to silently survey the defence system of the fort and the condition of Aditya Verma's heir, the Crown Prince Neelsingh

Verma II. Even though it's a desolate princely state, it has good defensive measures to avoid attacks and make the Company's job even harder.

As per the Doctrine Of Lapse any kingdom that is without an heir and the current ruling monarch is dead, the kingdom can be annexed via the doctrine. We have been keeping an eye upon that kingdom for ages...anything that might help us to catch hold of that state for good.

Jhansi, another kingdom is under the same situation but except that the young king is not with an heir despite being married to his Queen, Rani Laxmibai. Rangarh and Jhansi are near to each other which is an advantage for me as my good friend Captain David Hollers is in - charge of the 15th regiment stationed at Jhansi, which makes life not too mundane as I thought earlier.

I must get ready to meet the Royal family tomorrow.

~ Cameron Lowell

Raina couldn't believe her eyes. " Dear gods, this can't be true! ....All that was said ....oh my".

She stuttered and re-read the entry thrice and kept her eyes trained on the name that was signed in the end.

She turned the pages to various entries, trying to see if whatever written in it was true.

April 17, 1848

Today was the starting year in India as the new commanding officer of Rangarh and I have been insulted by the Princess in front of....

April 18, 1848

Coming here was the gravest mistake of my life. I shouldn't have agreed to this. What is happening with me? I have no answers. I don't know why, but I'm starting to wonder if I'm getting attracted to Sagarika Verma. The woman has some kind of an effect upon me.....

The journal was full of entries marked with different dates belonging to another life. It was an old one and Raina knew it. Almost dating more than a hundred years. But what she couldn't believe was the owner of this journal and it's clues to history thought to be long lost by the citizens of Rangarh.

" How did this even come in my possession. I thought this was long lost", Raina suddenly gasped and collapsed on the bed as flashes of unfamiliar scenes that yet felt so familiar captured her eyes for good. A swirl took her mind to the past memories of April 17, 1848.

II. Memories of a dead past

April 17, 1848

"Sagarika, please, it's almost time for the angrezis to arrive at court", a frantic Sulekhadevi shouted through the closed doors of a Princess's chambers.

Sagarika Verma, the Princess of Rangarh ,was trying to shut out the voices of her lady - in - waiting by stuffing her ears with a giant pillow. Sulekhadevi finally managed to pry the doors open and strode in with a frown marring her soft features.

" Rajkumari ji, what are you doing? The angrezis might arrive any time now and you're here throwing tantrums like a small child", she chided a woman in an elegant gold and black lehenga, seated on a corner of the bed.

" What a happy way to celebrate one's birthday. Those horrid angrezis are the perfect addition for my official arrival at the court", Sagarika grumbled with a frown matching that of Sulekhadevi.

Sulekhadevi sighed as if she had heard this argument before and explained in a much softer tone then earlier.

" I understand your grievance , Sagarika but what can we do? If we don't abide by their laws then our kingdom will fall into the same ill fate like Oudh, Chittor and those other fallen kingdoms. Only the gods will know the time when we'll attain azadi".

The doors again burst through only this time it was the Prince Of Rangarh himself, Rajkumar Neelsingh Verma.

" Is she content yet"? Neelsingh asked in a huff. Sulekhadevi bowed her head in his presence and replied, " No, Rajkumar ji. The Princess is reluctant in meeting the angrezis".

" Bhaisa, I don't crave to see their chalked up faces so you can tell father to proceed the meeting without my presence", Sagarika snapped and crossed her arms over her chest.

" Sagarika please listen! I am the future of Rangarh and if the angrezis find anything that might offend them then Rangarh is almost considered dead! They might augment the price of the taxes, besides it's said that the angrezi officer stationed hither is new to here and we might not but be on our best behaviour as we no nought of this officer. Anything might offend him " Neelsingh explained in an exasperated tone.

Sagarika rolled her eyes and said, " That's Wonderful". At this Neelsingh and Sulekhadevi shook their heads at her adamant behaviour.

Neelsingh almost lost his cool at his younger sister's antics but calmed down after seeing Sulekhadevi's stern look.

" Please, at least for my sake or better yet...for Hindustan's sake, you must arrive at court. This is something you'll never hear me say .... I'm begging you"! Neelsingh clasped his hands into prayer position and pleaded with his sister in a mocking manner.

Sagarika rolled her eyes whilst letting a small smile play on her thin lips, she agreed to come to grace the angrezis with her royal presence , as she proclaimed, just for her brother's sake.

The Royal Courtroom was decorated majestically for the arrival of the British battalion or, as Sagarika liked to say, her official arrival at the court-room. A Princess in Rangarh was allowed to be present at the courtroom during important events only when she attains the age of seventeen, while for a Prince, being ten years old was more then enough.

Sagarika longed to be present at the courtroom ever since her brother was eleven, but she was denied every time by her father, Maharaj Aditya Verma. But now the situation that she was thrown in was not pleasant at all.

She hated the Britishers ever since her best friend Sulekhadevi's father was killed by a British soldier when he protested to pay taxes to the company. Her mother died due to leprosy when Sulekha was just twelve, she was later taken by the Royal family so that she could serve Aditi as her lady - in - waiting since the girl's father was in the Royal guard.

Though Sulekhadevi never admitted this in public due to fear, she hated the Britishers as much as Sagarika did. One of the horrific things that she witnessed during a stroll through Surajgarg kingdom were the brutal shootings by some British red coats after a few remote villagers rebelled them. Stories of looting wealth from Hindustan were frequently recited by Sulekhadevi to Sagarika and Neelsingh.

Queen Shanti rushed towards her daughter and fussed about the late appearance in the courtroom. " Where have you been? The angrezi Resident officer was seen arriving through the streets with an entire army. He already terrorised some of our subjects while arriving," she hissed .

" I was a bit late in my dressing, mother", Sagarika lied in order not to get any more negative attention from her mother. The king, Maharaj Aditya

Verma cleared his throat loudly to interrupt the mother- daughter argument and signalled towards the court's entrance.

A blond man wearing a red coat marched in the courtroom with a strict posture and announced , " Captain Cameron James Lowell is arriving at court with his battalion."

Just as he announced an entire army of British people in red coats and white vests marched in. In the middle a young man with dark raven hair and intimidating cold hazel eyes marched forward to the Royal Family while the others stayed three steps back expect for the blond man who announced their arrival, stepped along with the dark haired British but stayed a step aback from him.

Sagarika presumed that this was the new angrezi officer in charge of the administration in Rangarh, Captain Cameron Lowell.

King Aditya Verma, Queen Shanti, Prince Neelsingh and Sulekhadevi bowed their heads at his presence." Welcome, Captain Lowell," Aditya Verma said in a begrudgingly tone. Cameron gave a curt nod to him but fixed his gaze on Sagarika.

Seems that she was the only one that didn't bow before him. Cameron expected her to bow in front of him but the Princess just held her gaze and looked straight in his eyes which made Cameron to narrow his eyes at her. The king and queen noticed that their daughter wasn't bowing, this made them both to sweat profusely in front of twenty - six British soldiers and their entire court members.

" Sagarika , bow", Queen Shanti and her husband hissed at her but Aditi refused.

" hehe, the Princess is very naïve ,sire. She doesn't know that one must bow their heads before Lord Cameron," the blond announcer chuckled.

Though Cameron wasn't amused but still gave the Princess a strained smile, " No matter how naïve she is, everyone must bow before Captain Lowell. Tell her to bow". He gritted.

" No." Sagarika replied firmly and took a step towards Varian, " This head will not bow before anyone nor will it be lifted up in vain."

The Princess and the Resident stared into each other's eyes challengingly. The atmosphere grew tense like a ticking time bomb.

Cameron scoffed and looked at her in a menacing stare equally as she did, "I never forget those arrogant eyes that challenge me."

" I assure you, Princess. This head will bow to me one day. Hmph, this fear that your subjects and your family have, is the one thing that's ruling over Rangarh"! Cameron's deep voice sneered at her and turned towards the King and Queen with contempt laced in his eyes.

The entire court, British and Indian were all looking quite shaken up at the heated interaction between Captain Cameron and Princess Sagarika. Never in their lives have they seen such disobedience or defiance against the British by a Royal member from the very place they have indirect control.

Aditya Verma gestured for a servant to bring forth a huge trunk filled with gold coins for paying away the tributes. Cameron however still had his eyes over Sagarika that were filled with anger, humility and curiosity that someone had dared to question his authority, much less a women.

Instead of receiving it by himself, Cameron ordered the blond man from before to collect it from the servant much to Sagarika's annoyance. Once handed over Cameron turned his back in a swift move and barked out his orders in a strapping tone, " BATTALION MOVE".

Sagarika glared at his retreating back but inside she felt a burning desire to drive a sword through his body. The court members shook their heads and dispersed after witnessing the bone chilling event between their Princess and the British Resident.

Aditya Verma turned towards her and glowered, " You do realise what you did, do you?...to do something like this? You're lucky that you're still even alive after what you did"!

" I'm not frightened of him"! She glared back at her father. Aditya could only sigh, " Rebelling against the angrezis would only result in carnage and the loss of our Kingdom in the hands of those vile firangis. A member of a Royal family must always put the welfare of their Kingdom before their own ego. Understand that".

" How? By living in fear and mercy of those firangis who don't even belong to this soil," Sagarika defiantly asked narrowing her eyes at him.

Aditya Verma trembled with rage and walked off with Shantidevi following his lead before throwing her daughter a disappointed look. Neelsingh opened his mouth to say something but shut it off instantly and followed his parents out.

" Join on, let's go to your chambers," Sulekhadevi ushered Sagarika out quietly with a neutral look on her face. On reaching the Royal chambers she slammed the door which made Sagarika flinch.

" Hear me, Sulekha I'm so-", Sagarika started off but Sulekhadevi stopped her , " Are you kidding me? THAT. WAS. AWESOME!" She jumped excitedly and hugged Sagarika.

" You should have seen that angrezi's face! He was absolutely baffled at your reply! Hey Krishna, your mouth could land you in a great trouble do you know that"? Sulekhadevi's faced morphed into that of annoyance after praising her for the first two seconds.

" Oh my,thanks", Sagarika said sarcastically. Her lady- in - waiting shook her head and opened her hand to reveal a small envelope that had a red seal on it. Sagarika looked at it and raised her eyebrow at her friend.

" Oh it's your letter! It's from Laxmibai"! Sulekhadevi exclaimed as if it was the most obvious thing.

Sagarika's eyes widened, " Give give give. Oh dear, Laxmi didn't write to me for a longtime". She took the letter from Sulekhadevi's hand and sat on her bed leisurely opening the letter and reading it's contents.

Dear Sagarika,

It's been a long time since I've wrote to you and I have a perfect reason for it. The angrezis have been eyeing Jhansi for a longtime and I had to manage things in my kingdom for a while.

Gangadhar had been sick and everywhere it's chaos. I don't mean to worry you with the matters of my Kingdom so let's get to your birthday. First of all, many many happy wishes for your special day in your special life and I hope that you have many joyous years to come by and a long life to live.

Hope you are alright and so is everyone in Rangarh. Are the firangis bothering you in any way? If so do let me know and I'll always be there for you. I've sent your birthday gift to Sulekhadevi and I'm sure you will love it. Be safe and strong ,my dear Sagarika I know you will. Do send me your reply as soon as possible through letter and I hope we will meet someday.

With love,

Laxmibai

" Read your letter? Here's your gift from the lady", Sulekhadevi brought in a small silver box and handed it to her.

On opening it ,Sagarika found a beautiful ruby and gold necklace given by her friend, the Queen of Jhansi, Rani Laxmibai.

" It's beautiful", She cooed. " I'll send her a letter but I'll do it after I clear my mind of that awful incident. It was my first time at Court and it turned into a disaster."

Sulekha nodded in agreement her face made it clear that she didn't want to talk about anything that happened a few minutes ago.

"I'll sneak out my horse for awhile. Don't let anyone know I'm out", Sagarika ordered her and strode out of the Gulab Mahal.

iii. The heart and the mind

The sky of the kingdom donned a rich hue of vermilion as the sun started to set behind the horizon. Trees rustled it's leaves in the gentle evening breeze, birds chirped and started returning to their nest for the night. It was a beautiful environment that Sagarika's horse admired and loved as it ran on his four legs along the city.

The forest's calmness helped to soothe Sagarika's mind, it relieved her temporarily of the aftermath of the morning's disturbance. Wind whipped through her open tresses as her steed galloped in the colourful kingdom.

The ochre and blue fort came into view and she quickly pulled her stole even tighter around her head and blocked all the emotions from showing up on her facial features, like a true royal, her mother would say.

The guards, gave her a curt bow to show their respect for the royal and opened the fort door to let her pass through, she immediately breathed a sigh of relief when the guards posted there were the ones that were loyal to her as she knew that if it were the others, they'll surely report it to the King and the King will report it to the Queen who'll pester her about her absence.

Slowly Tara, her horse, trotted towards the stable and let Sagarika get back on her feet. The stable attender had already filled the horse's water bowl and closed its stable door.

Aditi had to sneak inside the palace to get back to her room as none of her family members knew she had been outside till sundown and she definitely didn't have the courage to face their disappointed faces.

Crawling behind pillars and using the other corridor which wasn't so frequently inhabited, she managed to reach her room and shut the doors before collapsing on the soft mattress. Sulking in her own thoughts helped the Princess to recover from any traumatising event.

Her family's cowardice and submission towards a foreign race made her blood boil with anger, even worse was that neither her family nor her subjects supported her when she stood up to the arrogant officer. They were all silent spectators.

Knock. Knock. Knock

Someone pounded against the chamber doors, groaning at being disrupted from her thoughts, Sagarika walked towards the door and raised her voice slightly and asked, " Who's there"?

" It's me,Sulekha, My lady", the voice from the other side answered. Aditi sighed, not wanting to meet anyone but since it was her lady-in-waiting she couldn't help but let her in, knowing she's probably called for or something important must be conveyed to her.

Lifting up the latches that locked the door, she let Sulekha strode in with a tray laid with fine food. By her actions Sagarika could tell there's something wrong.

The handmaiden closed the doors and turned to the Princess with an apologetic face. " The King and Queen haven't witnessed your absence but unfortunately they do not require your presence for dinner and....they aren't happy with the incident of today's morning."

Sagarika sighed and replied." I am well aware of the latter but... are they really that dissatisfied with me that they do not wish me for dinner?", she asked incredulously.

Sulekha didn't reply but her silence conveyed everything. To say Sagarika was hurt was an understatement, she was miserable. And she blamed it all on the new Resident officer.

"You just finish your dinner and...don't fret about it. I'm sure they will be back to normal on the next sunrise, after all it is quite hard to stay frustrated at you", the older girl assured her with a small smile tugging on her lips.

"I really do hope", Sagarika chuckled half-heartedly.

Sulekha pursed her lips and left to let the Princess have her dinner in peace. As the latter went on munching on her native cuisine, she reminisced how horrible this day went and how it ended with her parents being disappointed with her actions though her heart tried to console her by saying that whatever she did in the court was absolutely right and it was her dharm to fight for her own nation and it's people, but her mind did not agree with her heart.

It constantly showed how wrong her actions went throughout the course of the day. They probably are regretting about letting me attend the court, she thought.

Even Neelsingh didn't bother to see her and say everything was fine like he used to—so even he was upset with her. These problems that she tried to stood up against instead made her seem like a villain in front of almost everyone.

She took the water jug from the tray to wash her hands on the small basin after finishing up her meal to retire for the night. The chamber wasn't an uncommon place for her to be as she was never out on the public for seventeen years and even if she had to be, it was always a palanquin around and atop her with a troop of palace guards around her.

Her chamber is where she was most accustomed to other than the library where she likes to be in the palace of Rangarh. Feeling disappointed with the day's events she decided to call it a day and drifted off into a dreamless sleep with only the hooting of owls breaking the silence of the night.

The warm sun rays poked Sagarika's eyes awake and Sulekha and bunch of other maids walked into the chambers to get the Princess ready for the day.

As Sagarika sat up on the bed whilst rubbing her eyes to get rid of any sleep left, The maids pored warm water into the bathing tub and sprinkled sweet smelling roses, lavender oil and kept sandalwood paste near the tub.

" Which garment would you like to wear today, Rajkumari"? Sulekha asked as she held two lehengas of blue and orange from the wooden closet.

" The blue one".

Laying the chosen cloth on the satin chair nearby, she helped the Princess undress and onto the water tub.

The maids used sandalwood paste and turmeric to clean Sagarika's body of any blemishes. Next, they fitted the lehenga on her which was sewn with the most comfortable and finest pieces of fabric with intricate designs fit only for a royal.

The perfumes and essential oils used were heavenly to smell. They filled the chamber with an aromatic essence enough to attract roses to bloom towards the Princess. Jewels and ornaments only highlighted Sagarika's beauty to an extent that would make even the celestial Apsaras to quiver in jealousy.

Sulekha led Sagarika to the Palace's dining room for her breakfast where her family were already seated, chatting with each other as the servants around the room came with platters laid with delicious food.

" Good morning, mother, father", Sagarika greeted them meekly as she took a seat next to Neelsingh.

Shantidevi sent her a small smile but Aditya Verma just sighed in disappointment and resumed his talk with his wife leaving Sagarika dampened at the sight of her father upset with her.

Neelsingh, who was quietly watching the entire exchange between his parents and his sister, squeezed Sagarika's right hand and smiled in reassurance ,this was enough to make Sagarika to brighten up.

Breakfast went smoothly excluding King Aditya's silence towards his daughter but her mother and brother's reconciliation made her mind divert from her father's cold shoulder. Being the second day after Sagarika attained seventeen years she determined to make it better than the previous day and most importantly she was determined to avoid contact with any Englishmen.

She wanted to explore and shop in the Kingdom's marketplace like she always dreamt of. It was her number one thing to do in her bucket list when she turned seventeen.

Sagarika gathered up enough courage to request her father for a trip outside the palace walls. The King begrudgingly permitted her with four conditions.

One: Sulekha should accompany you

Two: You must travel in a palanquin

Three: Never speak inappropriately to anyone ,especially to the angrezis

Four: The royal guards must be there with you in the Bazaar.

Sagarika didn't have any issues with the first and last ones as she definitely was going to let Sulekha accompany her at any point and with yesterday's theatrics she did learn her lesson and was going to keep her promise on avoiding the foreigners until the time was right. Jumping into wrong timings to show off your heroism certainly isn't going to make things any better. Although the royal guards tagging along was a condition that irked her.

She wasn't enthusiastic on the idea of having a trail of palace guards around her while trying to enjoy a day out in the kingdom with her lady-in-waiting after being locked up for nearly seventeen years inside the old palace walls. But she sighed and agreed ,just to have a normal day and also to patch things up with her father.

The royal Palanquin was ready with its lifters and four guards were assigned to go with it.

She did sneak out from the palace yesterday but that was only up to the nearby forest she was familiar with, seeing the entire kingdom was a treat for Sagarika. She didn't realise up till now on how the kingdom lived up to its name. The Kingdom's market was bustling as usual with its colourful shops and equally enthusiastic vendors.

Many of the citizens who were in the market stopped and bowed when they saw the palanquin and guards entering the marketplace. Seeing the others the rest of the occupants in the market too stopped whatever they were doing and tried to get a glimpse of their Princess.

" That must be our Princess".

" Oh my, she's a gorgeous woman indeed"!

" She looks much like the Queen"!

" No she resembles the King much more than the Queen"!

" Perhaps, but she does have her mother's eyes"!

"Oooh. I've heard that she locked horns with the new angrezi officer yesterday"!

"Seems like she isn't aware of the situation here. Who can blame a women who was kept from the outside world so long"!

"I am glad that we have a Princess who is brave enough to challenge those people unlike you lot. Show some respect"!

All the attention from her subjects did make Sagarika quite uncomfortable but she didn't blame their curiosity for even she would be eager to see the face of a person she has heard for a long time but never got the opportunity to see them, though gossip definitely does travel fast.

"Shall we have a look at the jeweller's crafts"? Sulekha asked as she pointed towards a shop of a merchant filled with glittering ornaments.

" Absolutely", Sagarika smiled and with that both the girls headed towards merchant's shop as the guards waited for them outside. A shocker for both of them was that there were already two customers in the shop. British ones on top of it. The Resident officer and an English women accompanying him were the sight that greeted them.

Before the foreigners could turn to look at the two women, they brushed past them without even sparing them another glance. The merchant saw them approaching and almost fell off his seat.

"M-M-M'Lady! What brings you here to my humble shop"? The merchant asked as joined his hands to pay respect to the kingdom's Princess.

Sagarika smiled and shook her head, " Please. I've just come here for my companion. There's no need for such formalities".

The merchant nodded and enthusiastically presented his finest pieces of jewellery for the two women to choose. There were a set of ornaments made out of gold, ivory, silver, diamond,emeralds and many other precious stones.

Cameron kept his eyes set on the Princess of Rangarh, he seemed to notice the girl properly ever since their first official meeting. Her hair was dark as the midnight sky and the locks were like tumbles of waves straight from the sea shores of Surat. Strings of jewellery studded with emeralds and diamonds, ran down from her forehead partition, a large nose ring adorned her nose which highlighted her entire face altogether.

Her eyes which were the colour of green jade, illuminated her olive face along with the rose - like lips. Princess Sagarika of Rangarh was indeed as beautiful as depicted by the rumours in the Cantonment.

The skirt of her blue lehenga brushed along the floor as she went past him, accompanied by a female he saw at the court the other day. Cameron was miffed at the ignorance of the Princess but he didn't understand the sudden attract he felt towards her. It was a very foreign feeling to him.

Esther, one of his companions from the Cantonment, dragged him along with her to visit the Kingdom's Bazaar despite his protests of overbearing works. Looking at the sets of ornaments certainly bored him to oblivion and the sudden entrance of the Princess and her friend created an interesting distraction.

"Is that the Princess"? Esther asked, leaning over to whisper in his ear.

Cameron's right eyebrow twitched slightly at the question, " Yes", he replied bluntly making Esther frown. The Englishwoman turned towards the new arrivals and cleared her throat nervously.

"Hello your Highness, I'm Esther Woods. Pleased to make your acquaintance", she introduced herself to Sagarika and smiled, hoping for an acknowledgement from the Indian Princess.

Sagarika and Sulekha turned towards Esther with confused expressions. They weren't sure as to why a British was suddenly making friendly talks when their entire race was at odds with each other.

Sagarika's lips stretched into a small smile as she answered back, " My pleasure. Princess Sagarika Verma of Rangarh and this is my associate, Sulekhadevi". Sagarika's hand gestured towards Sulekha at the end.

The honey haired Esther grinned at Sulekha, who was wary of the entire situation.

"Oh I know who you are! Your highness is quite popular within the walls of the Cantonment", Esther proclaimed with a chirpy cadence much to Sagarika's uneasiness.

"All good things I hope"?

The firangi girl laughed melodiously at the question. "It depends, Princess", she answered cryptically.

Sagarika and Sulekha exchanged dazed looks with each other but Esther continued her conversation, "So, may I ask why the Princess of the Kingdom, is here to buy jewels from the Bazaar when they can be delivered to the Palace itself"?

"I wanted to visit the Bazaar myself. I haven't seen it my entire life," Sagarika stated in a casual tone surprising Esther in a weird way. Soon both the girls were chatting with each other like long lost friends with Sulekha trying to exclude herself out of the conversation due to her lack of knowledge in the English language.

Cameron never thought he would see the rebel Princess having a civilised talk with a Britisher when she just scorned their presence the previous day. On the contrary, he expected her to sneer upon the white girl instead of entertaining her attempts at a friendship.

He was definitely infuriated by her words when she insulted his status in front of his comrades and the royal members of the court. The incident was too hard to digest, especially when he was quite eager to see her due to the flying rumours about the kingdom's hidden Princess. This prompted him to assume that her cold behaviour would extend even upon the warm hearted Englishfolks who admired the Indian culture.

Suddenly he felt unwanted and left out in the shop. Cameron contemplated wether on slipping unnoticed out of the shop or just stay back and pretend that everything was normal. Esther nudged his shoulder, disturbing his plans of escape. He scowled at her and lifted an eyebrow in question.

"Which one do you think suits me"? She implored as she held two necklaces made of rubies and sapphires.

"Honestly, I have no clue. Pick the one you like".

"Oh come on Cameron," she pouted. " Don't be such a bore".

He rolled his eyes at her, "Esther, I have no idea what on earth I myself am doing here so please don't ask for my opinions on such matters", he drawled and went back to ignoring everyone's presence.

"Esther, if I may?", Sagarika intervened from her place after mentally laughing at the angrezi officer's disinterest, "I would suggest you go for the sapphire one as the blue gems would compliment your eyes", she pointed out, signaling the English girl's azure eyes.

"Oh thank you, Sagarika! At least someone has taste", Esther giggled much to the chagrin of Cameron.

Sagarika laughed along with Esther. Cameron felt himself drawn towards her music like laughs just the way a moth would to a flame. He did not understand this sudden attraction towards the Indian Princess he thought he hated, her eyes which were challenging the other day, also seemed like pieces of jade which the Chinese used for their ornaments. In other words, they were alluring.

A soft smile crept upon his lips unknowingly as his hazel eyes gazed into the space while his ears stayed at the present.

Suddenly a voice in the distance woke Raina from her trance. She jerked up and looked around in a daze while trying to understand the series of unfamiliar events that played in her head.

"Raina! Raina, open the door! Why is it closed"? The voice which she recognised as her mother's, called out from the other side of the door.

Clutching her head she walked towards the wooden frame , and unlocked the latch to reveal a very impatient Shweta Yadav.

Shweta, her mother, placed her hands on her hips and gave Raina a accusing look, " How many times must I tell you to never close the door! What were you doing inside"?

Raina frowned and stuttered, trying to find a good reason, "U-Uh well.....I was..you know what? It doesn't matter cause I'm 20 and I can close my own bedroom door", she replied confidently only for it to crumble on seeing her mothers glaring face.

"Oh really? You are still a child until you get MARRIED! So, you cannot close the door as long as you're staying in this house", Shweta lectured her as she twisted Raina's ear.

" OW,OW,OW! I get it. I get it!"

Shweta let go off her ear, leaving Raina to caress it with a small pout on her lips. The older women shook her head and continued. "Speaking of marriage.... Your father and I found a perfect groom. That too in Delhi. His name is Aarush Mehra ". She conveyed the information excitedly, hoping to have the same expression from her daughter.

On the contrary, Raina did not share her enthusiasm. She was shocked in a not - so - good way.

"Ma! You know that I'm still in my third year then how could you even think of my marriage at this time? I still need some time! I haven't even opened my fashion line and you're already bringing this up".

Shweta waved her hand dismissively, " Oh please", she scoffed and sat on the bed corner, pulling Raina along with her, " You don't know the boy! He's a good fortune, I'm telling you. He maybe just be a two or three years older than you but Aarush is from a well off family. They have a software company in Gurgaon and I heard that he's also the CEO of it. A chance like that is hard to get so don't throw sand in your luck".

Raina eyed her mother warily, "How did you even get a proposal from him? I'm pretty sure big city boys like him don't even look our way".

"Mrs Lakshmi Mehra was one of my good friends in college. I heard that she was looking for a bride for her son and coincidentally your father and I were look for a groom and we already knew each other well so it kind of clicked that way. And also, they saw your photo and instantly took a liking to you", her mother explained it in a giddy cadence.

Raina sighed, she didn't know what exactly to think of the situation. She never met the guy, heck, she doesn't even know what he looks like. A complete stranger. That's what her parents are setting her with.

Shweta placed a hand on her shoulder and smiled, the kind of smile you would find on someone's face when they're trying to convince you so hard. " Think well about it. Actually, tomorrow afternoon itself the Mehras are coming over to see you. So, don't go anywhere during the noon", Shweta warned her and grinned as she stood up to leave. Raina stared at her mother with a shocked expression.

"When and how did you plan all this? A-And that too without my consent"? She paused to take in a deep breath, "Now they're coming over suddenly? Ma yaar...this is not nice".

One look from Shweta confirmed that Raina's arguments with her were going to be futile.

"Listen here. Your father and I know what's best for you. So, I suggest that you don't double cross me with this matter. The Mehras are coming tomorrow and that's final." With that Shweta shut the door off with a bang, but then she opened it a bit and left.

Raina sat back down on the bed with a heavy sigh. She was in a dilemma and after a moment of silence she decided that she had much bigger and complicated problems than this, like the unexpected flashes of weird dreams that appeared before she even fell asleep.

And all this started with that old diary of an even older person she thought she would never hear of again. Raina knew that these were the starts of a another new problem and they needed to be stopped before they could grow into something big.

The diary was still lying on the bed with the page flipped to the first entry of April 18, 1848. Raina took hold off it like it was some sort of deadly disease and tossed it into a table drawer.

Her head spinned and her heart signalled for unfamiliar dangers. The clock struck eleven and reminded her that it was too late in the night.

Heyo guys!

I did edit the entire book so I would suggest that you guys read the previous chapters too since I have edited them too. Changes may or may not be major but I would still advice you to read them too.

So yeah, that's the reason this update took longer than usual. Anyways, do let me know how the story's going and please, do vote and comment!

iv. Scars and Souvenirs

Raina paced around the hotel lobby with a disrupted mind. Today was the day the Mehras were coming over and she just didn't know how to handle the situation. On top of it, the weird dreams that depicted the life story of Princess Sagarika bothered her even more.

They were truly disturbing to say the least. A Princess, who was forbidden to speak about in the town and was forgotten by almost all the people in the country, suddenly is now having the memory of her life played in her head. And the journal of Cameron Lowell had mysteriously appeared in her possession.

The entire situation seemed like a fantasy mixed with mystery and Raina wanted answer but she didn't know how to find them.

She racked her brains trying to find a solution. None of them made sense.

She couldn't tell her family about this but she did know someone who could her help her with this.

Raina pulled out her phone and scrolled through her contacts. "Hello? Yeah it's me....come over to my house as soon as possible. I need you."

"Why what happened"? The person on the other side questioned in a confused voice.

"Just do as I say"! Raina replied exasperated and hung up.

A few minutes later, while Raina was hanging in the library with the old journal, a woman the same age as her walked in. She took a seat opposite to her and eyed her quizzically.

"What happened? Why did you call me in such a hurry? Is everything alright"? She asked with concern etched on her face.

Raina took a deep breath in and said, "Listen Gauri. Whatever I'm gonna tell you may come out as crazy and totally unrealistic but it's the truth. Please believe me. I really don't know what to do".

With that she explained everything from the discovery of the journal to the visions of Princess Sagarika. As she went on, the expression of Gauri kept changing and by then it was that of complete disbelief and confusion.

"Is this a prank? Did I waste my time coming here just for you tell some fairy tales? Go tell this to some five year old he might believe it", Gauri yelled at her angrily, thinking that Raina had pranked her.

"No no no! Please, it's true! Here look, I even have that journal of Cameron. It has everything that I just said. This is not a prank, Gauri. I'm just as confused as you are and I have hope that out of everyone you would understand better", Raina pleaded with her desperately, trying hard to convince Gauri that it was not a joke.

She handed the journal to her and showed her all the pages that matched with the visions she had. Gauri read them thoroughly, she didn't seem to believe it at first. After finishing the assigned pages, she looked at Raina with suspicious eyes.

"Are you sure you didn't write this diary in a different handwriting"? Gauri asked with her eyebrows quirked, earning an exasperated glare from her friend.

"Are you serious? Do you think I would waste my time writing a whole ass book in a very curvy - elegant handwriting just to prank you? C'mon! It looks way old and the ink looks very faded".

Gauri looked at her sheepishly, " Yeeaahh.... You have a point but I still can't believe that this all true! Especially Cameron's diary. You do realise that the guy was once a Resident officer here right?"

"Yeah I do, and apparently this guy had a crush on Princess Sagarika and she had one on him too", Raina said bluntly at which Gauri chuckled.

"Really? But all I ever heard of her was that she was a traitor to her king-dom and sided with the Brits. Oh Wow, this is taking an interesting turn. Maybe this diary can tell us about the real story of Sagarika and what really happened", Gauri suggested excitedly and made an attempt to grab the journal, only to be swatted by Raina.

"Probably....but I didn't read it fully", Raina stated absentminded as she played with the pages.

"What I don't understand is how did you find this? You know, if someone else had found it, it would have been locked away in some fancy museum. Maybe the one in the Fort."

Raina scoffed, "I don't want this this to end up in a museum! This may be some kind of a..key".

"Yeah huh. Archaeologists would die to get their hands on this but this is too good to let go", Gauri agreed as she stared at the ominous diary. She grabbed it from the table and began flipping through the pages furiously.

"Hey careful! That thing is antique! it could break apart easily" Raina cried out in fear, the diary was too dear to lose.

Gauri ignored her and continued her rampage on the diary, "The entry ends on March 26 1849, but the entry is incomplete....Like he lacked some kind of motivation or something," she concluded in disappointment.

Raina was about to ask something when she was rudely interrupted by her mother barging into the library. Shweta looked agitated and tensed, and when her gaze settled on Raina, it turned into annoyance.

"There you are! I've been searching for you everywhere and you're sitting here without any care in the world. Me being busy with all preparations does not mean you can sit idly and waste your time, you could at least get ready by yourself", She scolded her as Raina cringed at her mother's shrill words. Once she had finished giving Raina a earful, she turned to look at Gauri.

"Ah, Gauri it's a good thing you're here. Can you help me with a little favour, child?"

"Sure auntie."

"Thank you so much beta. You see, the boy's family is coming today to meet Raina and I'm very busy with the other things so can you just help her get ready? All the things are already set in her room", Shweta instructed and left in a hurry when she heard someone calling her.

Gauri turned to look at her friend with a teasing look, "Ohhh, who's coming? You never told me you were getting married"? She squealed as she shook Raina's shoulder.

Raina shook off her arms, " I never agreed nor did I arranged for this. Mom and dad made this decision without even asking me in the first place! Mom informed me about them yesterday night only."

"Oh", was Gauri's only reply, she didn't know how to handle this, after all her parents were pressuring her to get married too. She pursed her lips and pulled Raina up by her shoulders, dragging her towards her room.

"Listen, our parents and our society are never gonna accept a love marriage so the best is to marry according to our parents wish. But, if the boy is no good then you can reject him and ask your parents to look for someone else", Gauri advised her as she applied a layer of eyeshadow on Raina's eyelids.

"At least we can do that", the Yadav girl muttered.

Gauri shook her head and continued, " Whatever be the case, these big city boys must have someone girlfriend or other, they might have been forced too so......."

Her voice droned out and everything around Raina blurred as if she was going in a trance. Her eyes stared out in the space but her mind couldn't register anything that was happening in the present.

July 21 1848

"We have set an alliance with the Sengars of Mihir. The Mihirraj has an only son, the Crown Prince Ishir Sengar, and they desire to have you wedded to the Prince", Maharaj Aditya announced to his daughter when she was brought to the Queen's chambers.

The news pulled the lights out of Sagarika's heart. She expected her parents to marry her off to some other kingdom but it was only three months since she was brought out to the outside world.

The Queen stared at her with a calculating gaze as she fiddled with her stole. Shantidevi was lying on her side on the diwan couch with her husband addressing her daughter. She was reluctant on letting her daughter being married off but she had no other choice.

"He is just a young age of nineteen and a brave,good looking lad, he will certainly be a perfect match for you," the King continued with mirth, hoping to sway Sagarika into the proposal.

"Besides, we want Mihir as our ally," Shantidevi interrupted and got down from the couch, making her way to where Aditya stood. " Mihir has a vast military that will infinitely help us in the time of need," she finished with a grave expression, indirectly indicating the 'time of need' to be the Britishers.

Aditya had a thoughtful look on his face as if he was finally seeing the bigger picture.

"You are right ,my Queen, and the only way to secure that is by your betrothal", he agreed, emphasising on 'your'.

Sagarika was overwhelmed with responsibilities, her chest tightened as her parents continued. She knew about Mihir, or at least from what she heard from Neelsingh and Sulekha.

The kingdom was near the foothills of Vindhya ranges of and was considered to have a powerful military presence with a nearly indestructible fort which has made the kingdom a huge target for the Company. They were a bit vary of the kingdom and were eager to suppress their power.

It was also rumoured that Mihir was engaged in illicit and banned activities that the royal families of India have long abandoned. Sagarika wanted to ask her parents why after knowing the kingdom's infamous reputation, were they hell bent on forging a relationship with Mihir.

Instead she asked, "Tis is all so sudden, may I have some time to regard it over? Please?"

Aditya and Shantidevi exchanged looks with each other and looked back at their daughter, however it was Shantidevi who broke the pregnant silence.

" You may". Sagarika sighed in relief and made her way out of the Queen's quarters. She felt like crying until her eyes were deprived of water but she couldn't, she couldn't afford to let anyone see her cry in a helpless manner. She hated the sympathetic and fake looks of concern people would give. It made her feel uneasy.

She ran over towards the royal gardens and breathed out, releasing the constricting weight on her chest. The calming air of the palace gardens soothed her agitated mind and provided temporary peace.

The gardeners and servants present in the garden , bowed their heads in respect towards Sagarika. She acknowledged them with a nod of head, gesturing them to resume their work.

Sagarika walked around the garden admiring the beauty of nature that flourished within the fort gates. The gardeners have definitely made a paradise on Fort gardens, she wondered how much they were getting paid for their immense efforts. She hoped it was enough for their needs.

As she walked through, a red rose bud caught her attention. It was fluttering in the evening breeze and stood out brilliantly among the dull thorn vines. Sagarika was immediately attracted towards it, like a bee to nectar.

The rose vines crept around an arch giving it an elvish look. Sagarika reached out to pluck the lone rose bud but recoiled instantly, hissing in pain as the sharp thorns pricked her delicate fingers.

"You ought to be careful, miss. The thorns, though not poisonous, can cause infection."A new voice filled with foreign startled her badly. She turned her head so quickly that her neck would have snapped from the force.

Her eyes met with a familiar shade of hazel belonging to Captain Lowell. She wasn't surprised to see the angrezi there since his presence in the fort had been quite frequent. She had often heard her father and brother speak venomously about his intentions on the throne of Rangarh and now being face to face alone with him, made her jittery.

"You mustn't worry about my well being. A few ointments should be enough", she replied curtly as she observed the bloody pricks that had turned pink.

Cameron smirked in response and shifted his gaze towards the flower, with a swift move he separated the rose from its plant , his hands unscathed unlike hers.

"How didn't you get hurt"? Sagarika asked innocently, her green irises searching for a scratch on his pale hands.

Cameron chuckled at her question, "It requires skills, Princess", he said as he toyed with the rose stem. Sagarika's hand reached out for the flower but the Resident tugged his hand away slightly. Sagarika to furrowed her eyebrows in confusion.

"Not so fast", he tutted and inched closer to her. Sagarika's heart ran faster than usual, her breath became ragged. Cameron brushed a hair strand from her face and tucked the rose behind her right ear.

The gesture stiffened her body.

Cameron's fingers trailed the side of her face gently as he pulled his hand away. He noticed that her cheeks coloured and her eyes refused to meet his.

On the other hand, Sagarika prayed that no one noticed her rendezvous with the Resident or she was surely going to pay a hefty price for it.

Regaining her consciousness she stuttered, "Um...Uh..please, pardon me ..I must take your leave".

Cameron, who was silently observing the effect he had on the Princess, smirked and bowed mockingly with his hand motioning her to move on.

Sagarika hesitated for a moment before running away from the Captain with a palpitating heart. The rose given by him was still tucked away in her dark tresses emitting a divine fragrance. She ignored the stinging pain in her fingers as she navigated her way through the palace corridors.

Over the past four months, she and Esther became fast friends, they hung out whenever they could in the woods and at times Cameron would accompany her, usually out of his will. Either Esther was clueless or she just loved tormenting him.

Sagarika got used to his presence from both the court meetings and Esther. The two would occasionally exchange a conversation, which were mostly petty arguments that Esther loved to witness. No one except Sulekha knew about their friendship and they decided it was best that way.

As Cameron watched her go, his sergeant, Sebastian Wayer, came to his side. Sebastian saw Cameron's eyes glinting with amusement, he followed his Captain's gaze and saw the Princess capering off in a hurry.

"Say, Sebastian. What do you think of the Princess"? Cameron's voice averted his attention from the Indian woman. Sebastian looked back at him with a bewildered look.

"Um... that she is a dainty damsel that has no respect whatsoever for the Company and the Crown"? He replied inconspicuously with confusion in his cadence.

Cameron laughed abrasively at his reply, "Yes. Yes she is".

"I don't seem to understand this sudden curiosity of yours, Sire. What is that you have in your mind"? Sebastian asked carefully.

"Nothing."

Sebastian analysed his friend keenly, a shock ran through his eyes, "Oh dear God", he sighed rubbing his temples, "Sire she's an Indian! And a Princess of the kingdom that the Company badly wants to annex. You mustn't sully your duty with such things".

Cameron's eyes flicked back to him, "When did I ever say of such 'things'? Follow on. We have court proceeding to attend".

Saying so in a cryptic way , Cameron turned his back and headed towards the Palace entrance followed by a suspicious Sebastian.

With that the vision dissolved when Gauri shook Raina's shoulders, shouting incoherent words at her.

"Hello? You in there? Raina, what happened to you"?

"Huh"? She jerked up from her trance like state and squinted her eyes to adjust to the surroundings.

Gauri snapped her fingers in front of her friend's eyes, "What the hell happened? You okay?"

"Ri, I just had one of those crazy visions again", Raina breathed out.

Gauri's expression changed. Her eyes widened and she looked at her in surprise. Her curiosity was peaked and she forgot all about her surroundings.

"Tell me everything! What did you see this time"?

Raina pursed her lips. "Um-"

"Raina! Are you ready yet"? Someone cuts her off rudely before she could reply. A young girl in a green kurta marched inside with her long braid swishing by her waist.

Raina's eyes shifted towards her side to glance upon her cousin. Before she gave her a reply, Raina caught a glimpse of herself in the mirror. She was decked up in a plain satin saree of lavender with golden jewellery glinting upon her neck and ears. Her hair was done in a messy ponytail with ringlets in the end and her eyelids were painted a dark shade.

An ordinary eye, may have perceived that Raina was fortunate to be decorated in such an extravagant fashion but the way she felt was like that of a goat being bedecked for a sacrifice. Or in her case, she was being sold off like a mare.

She fixed her gaze back at her cousin and said, "Yeah Sheela. I am ready".

Sheela didn't seem to take her tone into consideration as she advised her, "Chachi said to only nod or shake your head when asked a question, and to not mess anything up by saying something stupid. Also, she wants you to agree to this proposal and in no way upset the boy's family".

"Yeah..whatever....tell my mom that I'm not going to do anything stupid", Raina replied sarcastically, waving her hand dismissively at her.

"Well, they're asking you to come....good luck", Sheela said and beckoned her sister to move forward. Raina looked back at Gauri to see her smiling back at reassuringly.

She inhaled shakily and walked along with Sheela as a part of her mind was still lost, trying to decipher the vision that came fresh today, and the other part was trying to remember Gauri's advice.

The latter stood back in the room with her fingers caressing the diary and her eyes, kept trained on Raina's disappearing back .

Heya folks,

I know it was a very long time since I updated but I had exams going on and totally didn't have the time to finish this. Anyways, I've finally found the faceclaims for our two protagonists, Raina and Sagarika.

Raina Yadav played by Pranali Rathod

Princess Sagarika Verma played by Tejasswi Prakash

Let me know about the castings in the comments! The other characters are left to your imagination. And do not forget to vote, just click that little star button above.

v. Embrace for Impact

Raina's palms started sweating and her fingers fiddled endlessly as she made way to the drawing room. The tension was so thick that it could be cut with a knife. Her family and the Mehras were crowding the room, and when she entered hesitantly, all eyes turned towards her.

Her voice got caught in her throat when she noticed their fervent gazes rested upon her. Sheela gave her shoulder a squeeze in reassurance.

Raina plastered a fake smile on her face, "Namaste", she greeted them with joined hands. The Mehras smiled and nodded in acknowledgement. At this, Raina immediately retreated to a chair near her mother and clasped her hands tightly.

"So this your daughter? She's very pretty", a woman, whom she assumed to be Lakshmi Mehra said.

A warm colour coated Raina's cheeks when Mrs. Mehra complimented her. The family indeed looked wealthy and urban from their jewels to their accents. The sole purpose for whom the Mehras came all the way from

Gurgaon, Aarush Mehra, was sitting silently and watching her with intense eyes.

He must have been at least three or two years older than her but in no way did he resemble a typical millionaire CEO in shiny suits and shoes. Instead, he was wearing jeans and a plain white shirt topped with a yellow denim jacket. He looked casual but his features were definitely regal from his perfectly styled hair to his honey brown eyes, and he wasn't bad looking either. In fact he looked charming, but Raina wasn't ready to be thrown in a life long relationship. She wasn't even sure if was his type.

The idea scared her, because once a girl from a conservative Indian family was married off....there was no turning back for her.

Divorce wasn't an option and the Yadav girl knew better than to judge people by their appearance.

"And what do you do for your studies"? Lakshmi asked her, pulling her from her train of thoughts.

"Oh um....I'm in my third year of BBA in Lucknow University", Raina replied meekly.

"Really? What do you plan to do after BBA"? This time Aarush asked her in curiosity, his eyes boring holes into her face.

Raina felt nervous in disclosing her ambition for her future in front of her entire family, scratch that— her joint family full of opinionated relatives and a family that she might be forced to be married into.

Luckily she didn't have to because her father came as a saving grace for her. "Maybe we should let the kids talk amongst themselves alone. You know, get to know each other"?

"That's a good idea. Let them talk with each other and we'll all talk about our next step", Mr.Mehra agreed with her father with a thoughtful expression.

"Well then Nina and Aarush, you both can go to her room. No one will disturb you there", Shweta stated and signalled Raina to be off.

Alright, she miscalculated. The idea of being alone with a handsome guy in your room wasn't exactly making things any easier for her.

Nevertheless, she was with Aarush alone in her bedroom waiting for an avalanche of interrogation. She saw Aarush eyeing his surroundings like a hawk. She couldn't blame him, her bedroom was average.

"We can talk you know", his calm voice resonated within the walls.

"Sure. You first", Raina laughed nervously.

The corner of his lips turned up as he took a seat in a nearby wooden chair, "Fine."

But his question knocked the daylights out her and she nearly fell out her bed.

"Do you have a boyfriend"?

"Absolutely not! My parents would trash me if I had one"! She almost yelled at him before abruptly shutting her mouth.

Amusement danced in his eyes as his lips tugged into a smirk. "Fine. Are you really interested in this alliance? Because I don't wanna force you".

Raina visibly gulped at his question. She wasn't interested but she couldn't back out from it either. Honestly, she felt the alliance to be quite conflicting.

"Are you"?

"Don't divert the question".

"I'm not diverting, I want it to be mutual," she lied but internally she was curious to his intentions too. She remembered what Gauri said. 'modern city boys like him might already have girlfriends and they hate the idea of an arranged marriage.'

Aarush shrugged. "My parents wish for this relationship ,and I respect their decision because it is them that I am where I am. So if they want me to marry you then that is what I'll do".

Raina was surely taken aback with his answer. Her parents too want this relationship and so did his. But unlike her, he honours his parents wishes, and that settled a deep feeling of guilt in her stomach.

"Oh", she uttered weakly.

"Now you. Do you agree to this"?

Raina sucked in a sharp breath. Mrs. Mehra was her mother's college friend, and the Mehras were definitely a wealthy family from Delhi whom her parents would gladly go heaven and hell for making her a part of their family. Aarush was acting on his parents whims and has agreed to the marriage. Her mind already played out the consequences if she refused.

She was stuck in the middle but that didn't mean she wasn't completely helpless.

"I...I", she hesitated before her conscience screamed at her to spill it before it was too late. " I agree to this marriage but I have a few conditions." She stated quickly.

Aarush raised an eyebrow at it. "What conditions"? He asked.

"Well, for starters,I still haven't finished college and I intended to complete my final year before marriage. Second, after BBA I want to start my own clothing brand and lastly, I must be allowed to visit my family at least thrice a year. If you have no objections to my conditions then we could go ahead", she said in one breath and looked straight into his eyes for his reaction.

Surprisingly, Aarush was very calm about it. Almost too calm for his own good.

"Are you done or do you wanna continue?", he asked politely, stretching his arms.

"That's it for now", Raina answered, oblivious to the sarcasm in his question.

"Good", he bit out sarcastically, that again, went unnoticed by her. Aarush continued, "I agree with your terms but I want to ask you something. Are you willing to live with my parents after marriage"? He implored her, his honey coloured eyes scrutinising her.

Raina scoffed, "That depends on how they treat me," she began seriously before chuckling at his slightly surprised expression, "Honestly, I live in a joint family so living with my in laws shouldn't be much of a problem".

"Don't worry, my parents aren't the clichéd in- laws. Also, this gives me much time for courting you", Aarush chuckled too.

☐☐ ☐·☐·☐ ☐☐

"We were friends from college first year, Shweta, do you think I will expect a dowry?", Lakshmi asked her friend incredulously.

"Arey no no, Lakshmi. This is not a dowry, consider it as a gift for accepting my daughter into your family". Shweta protested.

"But an SUV is too much,Ma'am." Mr.Mehra agreed with his wife. His eyes caught the forms of Raina and Aarush coming down from the stairs.

"Ah look, the children are back!" He exclaimed, diverting everyone's attention back to the pair. "I hope everything was alright? What does Raina have to say"? He asked but his question emphasising more on Aarush.

"I have agreed to this marriage", she replied half hearted lay but it went unnoticed by everyone when their faces broke out into illuminated smiles. All except Gauri.

"And what about you Aarush beta"? Raina's grandmother spoke for the first time startling her relatives.

"Fine by me", Aarush shrugged casually. Everyone broke into excited whispers amongst themselves.

"No what? It's only the girl's family that has to visit our home and then we can finalise everything", Mr.Mehra announced happily.

"Definitely! We'll try to come by next week if possible because...you know we have to manage the hotel and all," Raina's father, Roop Yadav, tried to compromise.

"We can understand. Please take your time, we have already grown fond of Raina and we gladly accept her into our family. We just need you to have a look around your daughter's future home", Lakshmi implied, flashing a grin towards Raina who had a deep red tint on her face.

"We're so glad to hear that, we will surely come," Shweta assured, feeling ecstatic that the Yadavs were finally joining the Mehra family.

Raina finally felt relieved when it was time for the Mehras to leave. She was a rookie in intimate relationships and being thrown into matchmaking situation in front of your family was the most awkward moment ever.

"Call me when you reach Delhi", Shweta told her friend as she saw their send off. Lakshmi nodded in agreement as she got into a cab.

Raina stood over in her hotel porch, anxiously watching them leave when Aarush turned to face her.

"Here. This is my number, call me whenever you want," He winked as he handed over a small slip of paper.

"Oh", Raina replied coyly but realisation hit her, "What about mine"?

"Not now. I'll ask mom", he answered smirking and left slyly before anyone caught him. Unfortunately, Sheela's sharp eyes never left the duo. She bumped her shoulder onto Raina's after the Mehra boy left.

"Flirting before marriage. Honestly, I've never seen you so shy before you're the most extroverted person in our family buuuut, looks like things are gonna change now", she said cheekily, dragging the u.

"Don't you have anything else better to do"? Raina snapped playfully before laughing along with her cousin.

"And miss the opportunity to mess with you? Hell no"! Sheela replied chuckling.

Gauri, who had been missing since the last two hours, appeared out of nowhere and pushed her way through the sisters.

"Excuse me", she cut in and dragged Raina away without waiting for a response.

"Hey what the hell"? Raina yelled at her, rubbing her arm from where Gauri caught her.

"I found a lead. I know someone who knew Sagarika and Cameron"!

AUTHORS NOTE

Okay ,you can yell at me and throw your slippers for not updating in a long time and also....well hehe .....leaving u guys with a cliffhanger.

Arranged marriages are quite tricky. Sometimes they're a curse and at times they are proven to be efficient, but for some especially girls, it becomes an obstacle in achieving their goals.

So if you ask me I would say that this concept is grey. It's not right and it's not wrong either, but it's negative results are definitely not acceptable.

Anyways, Vote, Comment and share this story. Just comment your general thoughts, constructive criticism and basically your views on this story. Add this story to your library for notifications whenever I update. Also do check out my new book Descendants of Crowns in my profile (perfect for Mahabharat , GOT and historical fiction fans).

vi. Dug Out Secrets

"I found a lead. I know someone who knew Sagarika and Cameron"! Gauri exclaimed, waiting for her friend's reaction.

Raina blinked.

"You're telling me that someone knows people whom have been practically wiped off from history"? Rain asked in disbelief.

"Um...if you say it that way then yes".

"Oh yeah? Who?"

"Do you know that guy who just joined the Army recently"? Gauri implored.

"Who? You mean Keshav Ranaut, the guy who used to flirt with you during our twelfth grade"? Raina said as she tried to stifle her laughter. Gauri rolled her eyes and groaned at the memory.

"Yeah yeah the same one. Anyways, according to Cameron's diary, Keshav's ancestor who might be his great great grandfather or something had met with Sagarika and this guy somewhere around December."

"Wait what?" Raina exclaimed, " How exactly is that even possible"?

"Because Cameron mentioned in his diary that Sagarika met with someone named Rajesh Ranaut, and Rajesh could definitely be related to Keshav because ....they're both Ranauts"! Gauri explained as if it was obvious.

Raina shot her a pointed look.

"Are you clueless or just clinically brain dead"?

Gauri's face morphed into that of a perplexed one. "Um...huh"?

"There are many Ranauts in India. Heck there's an actress with a Ranaut surname, are you saying that Keshav is the only Ranaut"? Raina ranted annoyed.

"Seriously Raina, don't you think I know that"? Gauri snapped, " Besides, Keshav's family has been known to be here longer than anyone, so it's obvious that Rajesh Ranaut was his ancestor"!

Raina pondered over what she said but Gauri's patience was wearing thin over her friend's obliviousness.

"Are you coming or not"? She slicked her tongue, waking her out of her thoughts.

"Huh? Fine. Just let me change! And Gauri, if it's not worth it then you had it", she threatened as she stormed back inside her room.

After she changed back into a much comfortable kurta and jeans, she found her mother arranging everything back in place after the Mehras left. She tried to silently sneak past her along with Gauri.

"Now where are going"? Raina cringed as she heard her mother.

"Um.." she tried to think of an answer when Gauri came to the rescue.

"Aunty, we're going to the market place, you know to find some outfits for....when she goes to Delhi", she said the last line quickly beforing flashing her friend's aunt a Cheshire grin.

Shweta looked at the two with narrowed eyes. Raina tried hard to conceal her expression while Gauri still had the mega watt grin on her face.

"Fine but do one thing, go to Ramu uncle's shop and buy 2 kg of atta along with it. I'm out of wheat for tonight's dinner and there's a lot of things pending ...." Shweta ranted on, without noticing the two slipping out silently.

"Understood"? She finished and turned around to find the place deserted.

"Kids these days! I don't know how she's going survive with her in -laws. God knows"! She harrumphed, shaking her head.

Gauri had a hard time navigating through the narrow lanes of Rangarh with her scooter. Raina sat behind her, her ponytail blowing in the hot summer air.

"By the way, what did your vision say", Gauri asked remembering the time Raina's eyes glazed over. Raina sighed and told her friend everything from the alliance of Mihir and Rangarh to Sagarika and Cameron meeting again.

Gauri's face changed to a grim expression.

Keshav's house was a small one story building with green painting coming off from the walls. Raina got down from the scooter and rang the doorbell.

A young man with a crew cut and dark mischievous eyes opened the door. He was surprised when he saw the two girls at his doorstep, especially Gauri. He grinned at the two, "Hey! What brings you guys here?"

The girls were equally surprised at seeing him, "Hey, I thought you were in

"Oh um...is your grandfather here by any chance,"? Raina asked, ignoring his previous question.

Keshav knitted his eyebrows, "Um..yeah. Why"?

"We want to have little chat with him. Is that okay with you"? Gauri snapped but batted her eyelashes when she realised how sharp her tone was.

Luckily for her, Keshav didn't notice the edge in her voice because he said, "Sure, anything for you"!

Raina wished she had a popcorn with extra butter.

Keshav lead the girls to his drawing room and informed his mother about their arrival. Keshav's mother went inside her kitchen to prepare tea for the two. Meanwhile, Gauri kept fidgeting with her fingers as her past with Keshav wasn't very fun for her, it also didn't help that Keshav kept stealing glances with her.

Mrs. Ranaut came with a tray of tea cups and some biscuits along with an old man whom Raina recognised as Keshav's grandfather.

"Yes Beti, what was the reason that you wanted to meet with me?" The old man asked Raina and looked at Gauri, "And who's this"?

"Dadaji, that's my um...school friend Gauri", Keshav replied quickly.

His Grandfather nodded and signalled Raina to continue, "Uh yes sir, actually I came here to ask you if you knew anything about the former Princess here...Sagarika"? She asked cautiously as she knew that the late princess's reputation was not exactly favourable by the people.

Keshav and his mother looked at each other in confusion, before his grandfather could reply, a much aged voice caught their attention.

"Sagarika..." it croaked with difficulty, everyone turned to the voice's direction, a much old man than Keshav's grandfather entered the room hobbling with the help of a stick. Mrs. Ranaut rushed to his side and helped him across the room.

Gauri leaned towards Keshav and whispered discreetly, "Who's that"?

Keshav felt elated when she asked him, "That's my great- grandfather", he replied earning a look of disbelief from her.

After getting seated on a chair, the old man asked"What do you want to know about her"?

"Everything. I heard that your one of your ancestor met her once in the 1800s", Raina answered accompanied by a nod from Gauri.

"Ah yes, it was my grandfather who met her once. My father had heard a lot about her from him, though my Dadaji died way before I was born, my father used to tell me how he had met Sagarika when he was just a baby and how his father knew her very well."

Everyone listened to him with rapt attention. Gauri spoke for the first time, "What did your father say about her"?

He squinted his eyes and gripped his walking stick, "I'm sorry kids but my memory is very lousy these days, my age is catching up and I don't remember much about her". This disappointed the girls.

"But, I do have a precious heirloom that my grandfather passed down to his son and finally me." The eldest Ranaut got up with difficulty and went inside with Mrs.Ranaut helping him. The girls and the others sat in uncomfortable silence with Keshav's grandfather breaking it.

"Why do you girls want to know about the Princess"? He asked curiously which was quite surprising for them as most of the townspeople called her 'that Princess' with contempt in their voice.

Luckily, Raina and Gauri had an excuse for the question. They had anticipated one like this.

"Actually I have an assignment from College that I should research upon a piece of our local history by interviewing some. It's all part of our journalism class", Gauri lied as the grandfather nodded his head.

Keshav raised an eyebrow, "Journalism"?

"Yes", Gauri rolled her eyes, " I'm studying journalism and I thought a report on Sagarika might increase my grades for its uniqueness". She replied smoothly.

"Oh", was all he said.

Raina turned to elder Ranaut, "Sir, do you remember anything about Sagarika"?

The elder Ranaut furrowed his greyed eyebrows in thought, "Hmm...we didn't have a very close connection with the Princess but from what my father said, she did visit my Great - Great Grandfather twice. You see, at those times, our family was in a financial crises due to the heavy taxes by the King. Rangarh was in a subsidiary alliance with the British and maintaining their troops took a toll on the treasury and so the taxes had to be raised." Everyone present listened with rapt attention.

"Many families like ours suffered during those times. One day, those taxes reduced drastically. The Resident present at that time, lowered them. No one knew how it happened so suddenly, even the king was surprised at the Resident's benevolence. But what happened was never known to anyone. It was Sagarika who had convinced Cameron to reduce the taxes after she witnessed the poor condition of my ancestor. She was depressed when she she heard of the struggles the ordinary people suffered due to the taxes. She appealed to Cameron Sahib and the firangi reduced them on her demand. The Princess was a good soul unlike what they say these days".

Keshav and the girls were a mix of emotions after listening to the former's grandfather. Many hidden information unknown to them were unearthed by the aged man.

Raina asked the question that plagued everyone's mind. "If she really helped people, then why was she labelled as a traitor"?

Gauri and Keshav looked expectantly at the older Ranaut, who sighed before saying something that shook their entire belief.

"Sagarika was not a traitor".

Raina pumped her fists in the air. "AH HA! I knew it!".

"How? How did you know it"? Keshav asked.

"Because my dadi told me. She too believed that the Princess was innocent".

Before Keshav's grandfather could say anything, his mother and senior Ranaut returned back. The latter was hobbling excitedly with two parchments in his hand.

"I've got it"! He exclaimed as Mrs.Ranaut helped him sit down.

"Here you go. This are the paintings done by my grandfather for the Princess and the Resident". He said as he handed the parchments to Raina and Gauri for them to have a look. The girls gingerly took them in their hands and observed the paintings with astonished looks.

Raina recognised the portraits as Sagarika and Cameron's. The parchment looked old and was chipped at the ends, the colours had faded with time, yet their expressions looked fresh.

"How.....did....wow", Raina breathed in disbelief as she stared at the portrait of Sagarika.

The senior Ranaut smiled. "It was made by my grandfather. He was an excellent painter".

Sagarika had a vintage yet elegant look with a poised figure. Her regal features were sharp and the colours that were used to paint her jade eyes seemed to penetrate deep into her soul. She looked exactly like how Raina had seen her in her visions but the more Raina observed the picture, something seemed to jolt inside her.

She swapped the painting for Cameron's. His too like hers, had faded but the mysterious aura around him had not diminished with time. Raina was shy to admit it but he did look handsome, even for a guy who lived hundred and something years ago. Cameron looked ghostly with his pale skin and dark hair but the only feature that seemed to accentuate his unearthly features were probably his hazel irises that held a cold look which gave Raina the feeling of a rainy and damp weather unlike Aarush's warm honey eyes, that were calculative and felt like summer.

"My Dadaji was an accomplished painter back then", The senior Ranaut started explaining. "Due to taxes and competition from outside, many local workers like my grandfather were facing losses, that's when Sagarika asked him to make a portrait of hers. It is said that she paid him a thousand gold coins for it and we have been ever grateful to her for that."

"Oh..." Raina said as she slowly nodded her head. "Then what about Cameron"?

"Cameron sahib never visited us but my Dadaji had seen him around the kingdom many a times and he painted his portrait from his imagination. Like I said, he was an excellent painter that he could paint from his memory".

"Child, earlier you said that your grandmother believed that Rajkumari was not a traitor", Keshav's grandfather started imploring as Raina listened patiently, "How did she know that?"

Raina shrugged, "Dunno. She said it was a gut feeling".

"And that gut feeling is actually true. Sagarika was named a traitor just because she fell in love......in love with an angrezi", He said seriously turning the atmosphere cold. Mrs. Ranaut who stood silently all the while, spoke out, couldn't keeping her opinion in.

"Is that really true pitaji"?

Keshav chimed in, "Wait"! He exclaimed laughingly. "Did something like this really happen in this boring town"?

"Well Keshav, this is more than just a boring town. Of course she was labelled a traitor because the royal family was too ashamed to admit that their daughter had fallen in love with the enemy. That too someone from another country. Do you really think that people would accept a blasphemous thing like this when even today, youngsters from other castes or religions falling in love is still frowned upon"? The elder Ranaut scolded.

"Oh- well- um...",Keshav sputtered.

"So are you against it or..for it"? Gauri asked, still not understanding the intentions of the family.

The old man sighed, "Its a very controversial topic, child. On one side it does seem wrong, but on the other hand, it indirectly helped the kingdom from the excessive brutality of the British. Cameron was the Resident british there and being a Resident, he indirectly ruled the kingdom until the king kept paying for the troops. Their main job is to annex the kingdom by emptying out the treasury until the king is forced to give his territory as compensation, but because of the love for the Princess, Cameron lessened her cruelty."

"Yeah I mean.. it does seem fair if you look in that way but, did Sagarika really love him or was she doing this for the sake of her kingdom? I feel like she knew the consequences and knew how to play", Raina expressed after listening to the explanation by the former. There was a different angle to the folklore and she was curious to unravel it.

"Could be Raina, after all, it happened a hundred years ago and nobody kept track of these inside information. Our family witnessed it and that's why I'm sharing this with you but remember, the royal family and their associates made attempts to wipe Sagarika from history but because of few , her story has been surviving as local legends among certain families and we tell these to those who seek the truth. Although her reputation as a traitor is much far fetched", the elder Ranaut warned, his message seeping into the minds of others except his father, who had a serene yet glum look on his face.

"Some just don't want to believe the truth", Raina breathed out in frustration. The elder Ranaut nodded in agreement.

"Hmph, someone should give this to Karan Johar. He would make a lovely movie out of it",Keshav chuckled silently to Gauri, finding the story to be as absurd as a fairy tale.

Gauri glared at him and hissed, "Shut up".

"Alright, maybe Sanjay Leela Bhansali with Ranveer and Deepika as leads!" He exclaimed as if he found the thought to be amusing.

"Are you out of your mind? There's something serious going on in here and you think it's funny? Also Ranveer is an Indian", She whisper - yelled irritatedly.

"Fine Tom Cruise then or maybe even that guy from spider man home-coming".

"Coming here was a mistake", she thought as she shook her head.

"Thanks a lot of the information, sirs. I think we'll be leaving right now," Raina said thanking them as she handed the valuable paintings back to the Senior Ranaut.

"No, thank you for listening. It's rare here to get people coming to ask us about the town's history." Senior Ranaut smiled as he got up.

Raina mulled over her thoughts from what she got this evening. She never thought much about the Princess except for the stories her grandmother used to tell and the occasional times where she would be guiding tourists around the town. But ever since the mysterious appearance of the diary, she dug more around Sagarika's history.

Internet gave scanty information about her and most of the articles had just one word to describe her.

An ambitious traitor.

She gave up as she slammed her laptop shut and switched off the lights.

Sleep did not come easily to her that night. She tossed and rolled as voices of another vision troubled her.

"Wake up Sagarika"

AUTHORS NOTE

This chapter is dedicated to @Haldhar_Priyetamaa for supporting me throughout this story and being the first reader to comment and being an active reader.

vii. Dance Through The Graveyard

"Wake up Sagarika", Sulekha's gentle voiced called her out as she opened the curtains to let the sun penetrate into dark chamber illuminating it. A trail of maids followed her behind and started about with their work while Sulekha tried to wake up the sleepy Princess.

Sagarika groaned as she rubbed her eyes, "Let me continue with my sleep".

"Absolutely not Rajkumari. The royal tailor is here and you're still deep in sleep. Wake up and let me do my duty", Sulekha scolded her as she pulled off the duvet covering Sagarika.

"Everyone present is going to be an angrezi," Sagarika grumbled as she remembered the purpose of the royal tailor. An invitation was sent by the Resident for a Ball at the Residence that evening and her entire family had to be present there. Though Sagarika and Cameron were on speaking terms, she still disliked the Britisher.

The royal tailor was called at the Queen's palace for the fitting of royal dresses of both the Maharani and Sagarika. It was a tough day for the tailor as both the women were picky with their garments. Like most princesses of her age, Sagarika too was particular about the clothes she wore, and even more so after she made her public appearance in the wake of seventeen years.

It was the custom of the Verma house of Rangarh to keep the girl child of the family hidden from the public eye until she attains seventeen. It was the tradition for more than hundred years ever since the Mughals started attacking kingdoms on the basis of the beauty of the Princess there.

To protect both the girl and kingdom, the family adopted such a ritual that would prevent much public knowledge about the princess. When the princess turns seventeen, she's given a glance to the citizens and immediately married off to another kingdom. But with the times having changed, the rules were relaxed but not much.

"Your highnesses, this is the finest silk that I have procured from Kashmir. It is as soft as the clouds on the sky. Please have a look. Princess! This garment may interest you, it's made of silk and the embroidery is done with golden threads," the Tailor advertised as he presented a green and red silk with gold and silver embroidery to the Queen who was instantly invested in admiring the cloth.

The Tailor turned to Sagarika and placed a yellow stanapatta having embroidery designs made from golden threads that were studded with rhinestones, and a long skirt of the same colour with sequences littered on it. Additionally, he added a lemon yellow uttariya of silk.

Sagarika ran her fingers delicately along the fabric of the skirt as she admired it, the skirt had a darker yellow underskirt over which a transparent lighter one was added. The Tailor further suggested, "Along with this skirt there's an elegant kamarbandh that I have brought......Ah, where is it? Dasiya!", he clapped his hands and ordered two of his servants.

They brought a thin golden chain and handed it to the Tailor. "Here it is".

"So, do you like it daughter"? Shantidevi asked her from over the diwaan, the Tailor too looked expectantly at her.

"Well I suppose.....I hope you have some appropriate jewels with it"? She added at the last after being convinced by the clothes.

"Of course, Princess", the Tailor beamed and turned towards his servants. They obediently brought over a wooden case.

The case contained ornaments of different kinds. Sagarika chose a minimal quantity to remain comfortable yet fashionable for the night along with the golden attire. The Queen payed the tailor handsomely for his work and sent him off gleefully.

"Sagarika, no funny business there whatsoever. Understood"? Shantidevi warned her, hinting to the previous disaster with Cameron during her first meeting.

Sagarika sighed and nodded. Even she for once did not want to involve in a drama with the Britishers for a night.

Two carriages awaited the family, one for the King and Queen and the other one for their children and Sulekha.

The Residency was on the borders of Rangarh away from the native civilisation along with the Cantonment. The British always stayed away from the natives and occasionally came out just to stroll along the market places or in the forests for hunting.

They believed that mingling with the locals would give them diseases but they never hesitated to hire Indian servants for their convenience.

Neelsingh and Sagarika joked all the way, their laughs echoed in the carriage but the only sour person present was Sulekha. She never enjoyed any of the pleasantry of the Crown Prince and definitely did not entertain the idea of tagging along with the royal siblings to the Ball.

"Prince,Princess, we're here", she brought them out of their fun by gesturing out of the window.

Sagarika glanced out from the carriage window. The Residency was a Victorian Mansion with resplendent decor and lights set up for the evening ball. It was like a small estate palace, but that was convenient as the Resident himself held power that equalled the King in indirect ways. Thinking about it made the Princess's face morph into a frown.

The interior looked just as fancy as the exterior, with servants and guests bustling around the place. Most of them were Britishers but there were a few scatter of Indian nobility here and there, occasionally mingling with their European counterparts.

His royal highness, Aditya Verma, was having a discrete conversation with one of his courtiers as his family stood huddled nearby.

"The Resident Sahib seems to be feeding off of our riches, look at his home, it's just....too fancy! If this keeps on going then we would be soon ousted out of our kingdom"! Vikramsen, the high courtier of Aditya, eyed his rich surrounding in distaste.

"I have a plan Vikramsen, I'm going to forge an alliance with the King of Mihir. He shall help us if these angrezis start to become a nuisance than they already are. Do not worry", Aditya reassured while keeping a facade of a calm look.

"Do not worry!? What are you saying my king? The Mihir family is a sinister one, the gods know what they have been doing inside that dark fortress of theirs. I have heard that they still breed vishkanyas, a practice that was forbidden long ago . Do you really want the young princess to be handed over to those people?" The courtier exclaimed, aghast at the decisions of his King but at the same time, afraid of contradicting.

Aditya gave him a sharp look. "I know what is right for my daughter and I am well aware of the Mihir family. That's exactly why I'm keen on this alliance with them", Aditya snapped at him, making it clear that he wanted an end on this conversation.

Sagarika on the other hand, heard everything whilst on the pretence of being deaf to their words. She felt the pressure from her family increase day by day to give a word of acceptance to the marriage proposal from the royals of Mihir.

She was clueless on what to say, her mother insisted to accept it as there was no other choice for a princess than to marry for political alliance. Yet she wasn't ready to leave Rangarh.

Her train of thoughts were broken by the devil who approached the small cluster with an amiable smile. A smile that would seem genuine to the naive but to the ones who have seen the demon, it will appear cynical with a hidden agenda.

Cameron was dressed crisply for the event with a black tail coat suit and matching dress pants. His dark hair was left ruffled and sharp that yet seemed neat and perfect. The scent of his musk cologne wafted in the air complimenting the lavender and sandalwood scent of Sagarika.

"I assume the ball's not too tedious, your highness"? Cameron asked sincerely, but if one payed a close look, it seemed almost taunting at the end. And Sagarika noticed it, causing her to glare at the British.

"Certainly not. It's marvellous I must say and the house looks extremely splendid today", The king replied with the same sugar coated tone as Cameron. The atmosphere grew turbulent around the two sets of powers. Their faces holding smiles but their eyes, showing the true nature of hostility towards each other.

Cameron gave a nod of acknowledgment towards the Queen and turned his attention towards Neelsingh.

"Greetings Prince, hope the privilege of being the Crown Prince has not yet turned to a burden"? he asked, subtly dropping hints, his hazel eyes shining with concealed malice.

"I hope not, not before I ascend the throne," Neelsingh chuckled sarcastically.

"Right. Because being the king requires dedication and the tiresome amount of time to look after the needs of your subjects and allies. I'm sure your father would enlighten you upon that matter," Cameron stated as his eyes darted knowingly towards the old king who clenched his hands behind his back.

"Oh he has. He lectures me on that matter on a daily basis".

Cameron nodded whilst smiling stiffly, not before his eyes caught the form of Sagarika. The Princess of Rangarh stood quietly next to her brother and her lady - in - waiting as she tried to avoid his presence. But luck did not seem to favour

"The Princess seems dull," he noted with mock pity, " How about you join me for a dance"? That turned the already turbulent atmosphere, frigid cold.

Sagarika looked astonished by the request. She did not expect this.

'The nerve of this man', her mind fumed yet her face displayed that of complete silence.

"I - um...", her jade eyes glanced over to her parents, whose visage held that of helplessness. They were in a fix. Denying the Resident and humiliating him in front of his own men was not a wise choice and certainly a dangerous one. They already witnessed the consequences for the act that Sagarika performed when she was first introduced. Cameron raised the amount of tributes to be paid for the troops and ever since, never lowered them.

Shantidevi nodded in approval and beckoned her to go forward. Sagarika took his hand which was stretched out for her to accept.

Cameron's cold irises illuminated as he felt the satisfaction of trapping the princess in his vice.

"I do not know how to dance", Sagarika muttered as they moved towards the centre of the ballroom.

"Just follow my instructions and you'll be fine", he reassured as he wrapped his left arm around her slender waist as he held on to her right arm. "Place your other hand on my shoulder and take a step backwards".

"Now forwards," he instructed softly as the pair glided over the dance floor with a few pairs of guests waltzing around them.

She fumbled with the step movements at times, but pulled herself up to avoid unwanted judgments. Cameron whispered instructions in her ears while they were dancing which seemed more like a hushed conversation to onlookers.

"You dance very well, Princess," He complemented.

"I used to learn dance before", Sagarika replied whilst having trouble maintaining eye contact with him. It seemed almost absurd, because a few months ago she dared to look him straight in the eyes to reprimand him off. It was a feeling she couldn't understand, something was off and no matter how hard she tried to brush it off, it just didn't seem to go.

In short his presence overwhelmed her.

"I don't think they like me very much", she commented further when she noticed the envious looks of a few British women huddled in groups, shooting her angry looks.

Cameron's eyes flickered to the group and chuckled softly, "Don't worry about them. They're just being petty".

Sagarika gave one last look to the white women and shifted her gaze. That was to much negative energy radiating. As the waltz came to an end, Sagarika excused herself and went over to the table where Neelsingh and Sulekha sat together.

She grabbed a glass of water nearby and downed it in a second.

"Everything alright"? Her brother asked cautiously.

"Does it matter"? Sagarika huffed as she set the glass down. Neelsingh went silent.

Seeing the tense situation Sulekha interrupted, "Your friend Esther was here".

Neelsingh's head snapped to her side, "Who's Esther"?

"A friend of mine. Do you have a problem with that"? Sagarika retorted, irritated at the sudden question.

"Well I do if that's the name of an angrezi lady", Neelsingh shot back equally irritated.

"She's fine. If you don't like it then stay away", she lashed out haughtily and left the table in a huff before returning back briefly.

"Where is she by the way"? She asked Sulekha innocently.

Sulekha shook her head playfully, "Must have gone to the ladies room".

Neelsingh watched as his sister left in the pursuit of her English friend. He didn't know what to do with the unexpected friendship when Sagarika openly detested the foreigners for their uninvited stay in Bharat.

"What's with her"? He asked.

Sulekha shrugged in response. "Maybe she didn't like dancing with that angrezi".

Sagarika wandered the halls looking for Esther when she heard a servant call out to her.

"Rajkumari, I've been instructed to give this to you", the servant handed her a chit and turned around quickly. Sagarika had a frown on her face as she opened the paper. A note was written in elegant scrawly handwriting.

Meet me at the library at 10 sharp.

- Sgt. Sebastian Wayer

'Now what does he want'? Sagarika meet him once or twice whenever he would accompany Cameron to the court but they would hardly exchange a glance or two. To be honest, he was just as arrogant as his senior.

Sagarika wondered the reason for his urgent meeting with her and looked around for a wall clock. She saw a European woman walk past her and stopped her.

"Excuse me Madam, but do you what time is it"?

The woman stopped and thought for a moment before answering, "I think it's almost ten to ten".

"Oh, thank you so much", Sagarika smiled and turned on her heels. The door to the library was opened a bit, assuming someone was already inside she stepped in with a hitched breath. A man with icy blonde hair and intense grey eyes crouched over by the fireplace poking the coals with a poker.

"Lady Sagarika, I did not really expect you to come", His chilling voice rattled among the library walls as he stood up, smoothing his silver - blue vest of any crinkles.

"And yet I'm here," Sagarika deadpanned as she closed the door and stood inches away from it, ready to bolt out if something was about to go wrong.

"And yet you are here..." he whispered thoughtfully, ignoring the woman in the room before snapping back to the present. His unsettling grey eyes bored into her as he spoke in a serious tone, "I shall cut straight to the chase. Stay away from Cameron. You do not want to do anything with him."

Sagarika scrunched up her face. She stared bewildered at Sebastian before regaining her composure, "I beg your pardon? What are you trying to imply Mr. Wayer"?

Sebastian exhaled exasperatedly, "What I'm saying is that, I know of your affair between the Resident, and though it may seem harmless to you it's in fact, very dangerous for the both of you. I've seen the way he looks at you."

"What"!

"Yes, why else do you think Cameron chose you for the waltz? It's because he fancies you".

Sagarika looked at him in disgust and if looks could kill then the sergeant would have been six feet under.

"How dare you make such implications about the Captain and me! I ought to have brought such a baseless accusation to the attention of the king but I'm not going to do so! This is a warning sergeant, do not take it lightly. I shall not hear any of these anymore", she spoke sternly with a lump forming on her throat, before she could break down, she stormed angrily out of the library.

She wanted no more of the sergeant and his assumptions but a voice in her subconscious nagged her.

'But don't you like the firangi too'? It taunted her, being the same reason for the lump on her throat.

Sagarika shook her head and replied back to the voice, 'Shut up! He's arrogant and most importantly a thief who's planning to steal my kingdom through conceited ways. He's nothing to me.'

'You lie', it whispered back darkly.

She couldn't deny it, if she truly contemplated on it then it was true, something attracted her towards him like a sunflower towards the sun. And worst part? Her subconsciousness realises it.

"GAH"! Raina awoke with a gasp. She grappled along her bedside table until her hands got hold of a glass. Gulping it in a craze she took deep breaths to calm herself.

This was the third a vision of Sagarika appeared and each time it came it seemed like she was being drained of her energy. She checked for the time on her mobile. It was just 2:45 in the morning.

Sleep wasn't going to come to that easily now but her plan for tomorrow was set.

It was time to pay the old Residency a visit.

VOTE SHARE AND COMMENT YA'LL IT MAKES MY DAY AND I HONESTLY LOVE TALKING WITH YOU ALL. JUST COMMENT

ON WHAT YOU WANNA SEE OR JUST GENERALLY ABOUT EACH SCENARIOS SO WE CAN HAVE A DISCUSSION.

THE BOOK FEELS LONELY WHEN READERS DON"T COMMENT.

ALSO VOTE IF YOU LIKE THE STORY. JUST KILL THAT STAR BUTTON

viii. Painted Ruins

The Residency.

Built by the first Resident of Rangarh, Sir George Jamison, and used until the last Resident of Rangarh, Captain Cameron Lowell before it was annexed in 1854 by the East India Company under the Doctrine of Lapse due to lack of any heirs of the reigning monarch.

Now the Residency was a part of Rangarh's post office. Rumours went around that the ASI was trying to take up the old building under their wing to convert it into a tourist spot for its part in history.

Raina and Gauri stood in front of gates, contemplating about various thoughts. Raina seemed to have flashes of the Residency in a different aspect, an aspect where it looked more Eurocentric than how it was now.

The Residency building was bustling with courier trucks and vehicles parked outside the once resplendent gardens that served as Cameron's leisure grounds.

Gauri shook her friend's shoulder, "Are we gonna keeping gawk or are we gonna go inside too"?

Raina shook off her flashes and stammered, "Um..yeah...let's go". She gave one last weird look to the building exterior and stepped inside. The interior was a chaos with workers and people moving hither and tither, pushing around and standing in queues at counters.

"Madam, are you here as a tourist or a customer"? A worker came forward and interrupted them, scrutinising his eyes at them.

Raina glanced at Gauri briefly before replying, "Tourists".

"Then please head to the third floor. This is only for postal service". The girls nodded and moved towards the spiral staircase that was now coated with fresh paint but still retained its old structure. Not before paying a sum of fifty rupees each for tickets.

The third floor was filled with tourists as it was more spacious then the rest. Flashes of the Ball incident and other visions flooded past her like the water flowing from an open Dam. Raina stumbled subconsciously as she looked through each relics.

Letters, pens, tables and candle stands from the Victorian Era was displayed inside various glass cases.

But the one that almost stopped her heart was a display that Gauri frantically pointed at, "Raina look. Isn't that who we think it is..."

Her eyes followed the direction of her finger and her mouth dropped open at the sight. A portrait was hung on the walls encased in a glass display like the the other relics. It was none other than Cameron whose portrait was placed in the displays along with the ones of his predecessors.

Unlike Rajesh Ranaut's paintings, the Residency one had Cameron in his official British Army uniform, the Red Coat, with all his medals of honours hung proudly on his uniform. Even in this painting, Cameron eyes had his signature coldness but what set Rajesh Ranaut's painting apart was that the official one almost seemed alive or in Gauri's words, "A painting straight out of a horror movie".

Below the portraits of each Residents were their personal properties. Raina trailed her eyes to Cameron's but all that remained there were an old fountain pen, his Howdah pistol and his uniform, tattered and faded.

"That diary would have been here had it not been in your library", Gauri whispered.

Gauri was right. The diary would be one of the relics sitting in a glass display under Cameron's portrait had it not been in her library. But what baffled her the most was, how did it end up in her family's Hotel? And all those weird visions of Sagarika and Cameron from the British era started when she got hold of the old diary.

"I didn't know that the Residency had a museum at its third floor. Why didn't you tell me this before"? Raina asked, looking accusingly at Gauri.

Gauri huffed, "Me?! Girl, you're the one who acts as a tour guide to your Hotel customers. I should be the one asking you"!

"I thought this was just a post office, and to be honest, I haven't stepped foot in this place until now. Like who writes letters and stuffs when we have Gmails and internet"?

"Well this place is in the outskirts, do you think my parents would allow me here all by myself when they thought twice — scratch that....a hundred times to send me off to College? That too with my cousin", Gauri defended exasperatedly and muttered the last part under her breath in a spiteful manner.

Raina shrugged and moved around the room. A mahogany table stood against a wall with a silver plate that read.

Mahogany office table 1824. Served as work tables by the Residents.

She ran a finger through the edges of the table, dust particles sticking on to her skin as she swept past. An electric sensation rushed into her veins the moment she ran her fingers.

Her breathing constricted in her throat as the familiar feeling of a vision came.

Sagarika climbed down from her horse as she walked along the neighbourhoods of her kingdom. Her feet kicking along the dusty roads in a winter morning accompanied by Sulekha. The pressures from her family side urging her to give a response to the royal family of Mihir grew heavier.

But she kept delaying it saying that she needed time to bond with her kingdom before leaving it. The truth was, she didn't want to leave Rangarh anytime soon. Marriage seemed like a foreign notion to her when all her friends and family were right here. But most importantly, she had to ensure that the British don't try anything funny in her absence.

As Sagarika and Sulekha wandered about, an anxious voice perked up their ears.

"I've heard that the king has raised the taxes again. God knows what we're going to now. I can barely afford two meals a day with the already existing taxes", an old man spoke up from a cluster of men sitting together under a banyan tree.

"Your absolutely right. I am convinced that it's all the doings of the Resident sahib. If he increases the cost of the troops then the king is bound to increase the taxes, wouldn't he"? Another one replied.

Sulekha and Sagarika gave nervous glances at each other.

"Of course! The angrezis are looking forward to annex the kingdom since ages, this is just one of their strategies. If the king is unable to pay their costs then a portion of our land will be given to Company, and soon after the entire kingdom will be handed over to them in a silver platter", another remarked snidely as he warmed his hands over a makeshift bonfire.

Sagarika could no longer stay patient, she stomped over to their group and cleared her throat, "Sirs, you do realise that if there's anything bothering you, you could gladly convey it to the Princess".

Everyone stood up with a jerk a at the sight of their Princess. Beads of sweat rolled from their faces at the thought of Sagarika hearing everything about the King's criticism.

The one who seemed to be the leader fearfully joined his hands in respect and lowered his head, "Forgive us Rajkumari, we shall not speak of such blasphemy anymore. Please don't inform the Highness, we beg you"!

"Yes, Rajkumari please don't tell Maharaj. Forgive us for our careless mistake", the others along with him pleaded in chorus.

Sagarika wanted to laugh out aloud and declare that they were just overreacting for no absolute reason but doing so would be discourteous in front of her subjects, it would seem like she was deliberately playing with their emotions.

Instead she smiled slightly and reassured them, "Do not worry. I'm not going to tattle to the King, besides what's wrong in openly conveying your discomforts? That's exactly why we take rounds around the Kingdom. To ensure that our subjects don't keep anything to themselves! Please tell me what bothers you so that I can help you".

The group exchanged looks of hesitation amongst themselves in confining silence.

"There's no need for hesitation", Sagarika encouraged them with her smile intact.

The leader stepped forward, "Princess, my name is Rajesh Ranaut and since the past four days the King has increased the already existing taxes further. Tell me, what will commoners like ourselves do when the one whom we see as protector becomes the obstacle in obtaining our daily meals? I'm just a poor painter who can hardly afford two meals a day with the meagre number of customers."

Another interjected and said, "Rajkumari, the King is not be blamed, after all it's truly the fault of The Resident Sahib, Cameron, who keeps on increasing the cost of the troops's maintenance. It's all because of him that the taxes had to increased".

"Yes he's right Rajkumari, that Angrezi Sahib is the culprit"! The crowd chorused together. Sagarika raised a palm to calm them down.

"If it's so, then I shall try my very best to lessen your burdens. I thank each and everyone of you for bringing this issue to my notice", Sagarika promised, assuring the people of a sanctuary that she doubted she could provide them.

After the group dispersed Sagarika turned towards Sulekha with worry glistening in her eyes, "How did this happen"?

"Well it's not exactly that the King tells you everything", Sulekha shrugged in a matter- of - factly manner.

Sagarika scoffed, "Well what on earth do you expect me to do now? I've made a promise to them, I can't afford to break it"!

"That's not my problem. You're too reckless, Sagarika. You should be more careful on what you utter and to whom".

Sagarika glared at Sulekha but the latter was unfazed as she had a poker face with her arms crossed against her chest. "Not helping, Sulekha. Not helping at all".

An exasperated silence engulfed between them. Sagarika remained mum with one of her eyebrows raised accusingly and her lips were set into a straight line due to regret. She hated breaking promises and the ones who broke it too.

Both of them stared at each other with their eyebrows knit together until Sagarika exclaimed, "That's it"!

"What's what"?

"Sulekha, if I cannot talk to the my father then I surely can try to talk with the Resident! What do you say"? Sagarika asked excitedly, happy at finding a solution.

"I say....you're an idiot", Sulekha said, smiling sickly sweet that morphed back in to a sneer.

Sagarika shook her head, " I understand that it's a stupid solution but what can we do? I can't talk to my father about this but if you see it in a different way then it's actually Captain Cameron whom we need to convince. Sulekha don't you see? He's the root cause"!

Sulekha wasn't convinced, her lip was stiff as ever, " This is madness I tell you".

"We need to try, Sulekha. We need to try in the least, there's no harm in trying. I need to do this as soon as possible." Sagarika urged and continued, "I am going to the Residency now and I need a coverup........Sulekha, please go back to the palace and if anyone asks then tell them that I'm in the forest with my horse. Just try to keep them away from my track".

Sulekha was struck, she regained her composure and shook her head, "No no no. Absolutely not Sagarika. I cannot do this".

"Yes you will and I'm not saying this as your friend but as the Princess of Rangarh. I command you to obey my orders", Sagarika stated sharply, her words crisp and stern. Sulekha was now left with no choice. In true sense, she had to obey the orders of her Princess wether she liked it or not. Reluctantly she nodded her head and left on her horse, leaving Sagarika alone.

The Verma Princess swung her legs and mounted her horse, pulling on the reins. The last time she had been to the Residency was when the royal family were invited for a ball. Ever since then she had never set foot in that place.

Her horse took her on the path to the Residency, reaching there she was stopped by one of the guards.

"Who are you? Don't you know that Indians and dogs are not allowed"? The guard questioned her rather rudely. Judging by his accent and appearance, he was definitely British. The others around him guffawed mockingly.

"She probably can't understand what we're saying. Don't you know English"? Another taunted her in between his chuckles.

"Leave it gentlemen, that's a local women we're dealing with, they're too uncivilised," the one next to him jeered.

Sagarika scrunched up her nose distastefully at them. Her blood boiled as she heard foul discriminations against her from the tongues of the very people she despised, "Well I'm not any Indian, I'm the Princess of the Kingdom that's currently providing you shelter and money with, so I suggest that you speak a bit more courteously to me. Although, I understand that being polite is a rather difficult task for the British, is it not"? She spoke, in perfect English almost shocking the guards. Her cadence remaining gentle yet firm while admonishing them.

The head guard sputtered, his hands shivering around his rifle. "Uh...um. ..I-I didn't realise that you were t-the P-P- Princess. Forgive us". The others around him hung their heads, not being able to meet her eyes.

"I-Is there anything you need, my lady? What h-have you come for"? Another stammered as he asked, smiling nervously that failed each time Sagarika's smirk widened.

"Is Captain Cameron Lowell available"?

"Yes, your highness. What shall I tell him"?

"Tell him that Princess Sagarika Verma requests for his audience immediately." The head guard nodded and left, his subordinates leading Sagarika inside the mansion who kept her chin in the air as if she was the one who owned the place.

A servant burnt firewood in the fireplace for warmth and another one came and served her tea with biscuits which she denied right away. She was not in a mood to eat or drink anything here, not after the insults from the guards. She had never felt so disgraced ever, the rebuttal to the guards wasn't enough to patch her ego.

'Mannerless. Absolutely mannerless and they call us uncivilised'!

After a moment or so the guard returned, "Madam, Sire approves of your request and has asked for you. Please follow me".

Sagarika gave a curt nod and followed the guard, boring holes into the back of his head which the guard was very much aware of as he subconsciously gulped. The prospect of seeing Cameron again was not exactly a thrilling event for her but it was necessary for the well being of her subjects and she was ready to go to even hell for it.

The guard led her along a spiral staircase and onto the third story of the mansion. He knocked on a door which was followed by a firm response, "Come in".

The guard opened the door and beckoned Sagarika to go in before closing it from outside. Sagarika's breath shortened at the sound of the door closing behind her but what didn't help the situation further was Cameron's taunting smirk.

He peered at her with his hazel eyes looking colder in the winter season as his chin rested on the back of his hands. He was seated behind a Mahogany table with papers piled on a side and a pot of ink on the other. "To what do I owe this pleasure"?

"To your ridiculously high prices", Sagarika snapped, not moving from her place.

Cameron was taken aback, "My ridiculously high prices? Now what have I done to offend her highness"? He mocked and gestured her to take a seat.

Sagarika furiously pulled the chair back and sat, after taking deep breaths to calm herself she spoke serenely, "I need to talk about the prices that you have increased for the troop's maintenance".

Cameron raised an eyebrow, "Is that so? I thought that the king did not have any problem with it! And even if he did, why did he send you and not the Crown Prince or one of his ministers"?

"That's because the king does not have any problem and I came here on my own accord. It's the citizens who are rather perturbed than my father", Sagarika explained, trying to keep her calm.

"The citizens"? Sagarika nodded.

"Ever since you have increased the costs even more, my father had to increase the taxes to meet the financial expectations. This has only disturbed the common folks, especially the ones who cannot even afford two meals a day. I request you, please decrease the costs so that the King can reduce the taxes or else they'll all go hungry", Sagarika pleaded, her voice trailing off when she remembered Rajesh Ranaut telling her his woes with pain in his voice.

"Do I look like I care about the peasants, Princess? I just want the costs to be paid through any means and since you might not be aware of it let me enlighten you, if the King does not wish to pay through financial means, then he can surely give away a piece of land for the Company. But I'm not going to decrease the costs. Or he can give away the entire Kingdom, the burdens both on the King and the people would vanish. Of course your family shall receive an annual pension for your generosity", Cameron was blunt and impertinent with the whole situation. He did not care about the requirements of the daily people, why would he when he was just one of those who wanted to acquire her kingdom at any cost?

Sagarika's lips thinned at his statement, she did not reply. She understood that this was all a part of his and the Company's ploy to snatch Rangarh through crooked ways. Sulekha was right. It was meaningless to negotiate with him when increasing the prices were all intentional with respect to the King's royal financial status. The Doctrine of Lapse was one part of the medium, the other were the deployed troops themselves, inability to meet their needs would end in the disposal of the Kingdom.

She gulped the lump on her throat and spoke, her voice croaking when she proposed her last resort, " Wh..." she inhaled to compose herself , "What if I apologise"?

"Apology for what"?

"For the time when I......insulted you at court".

Cameron burst out laughing.

No, it wasn't one of amusement but rather sardonic. Sagarika was shook and confused at the same time.

"You- you want to apologise? Seriously"? He asked in between his laughs. Sagarika glared at him, "It's not funny. I genuinely mean it".

Cameron stopped laughing, he leaned across the table, "Fine then apologise".

"I—", Sagarika hesitated, it was her ego that screamed at her to not apologise. It was not her fault, it was him who acted haughtily at her but this was a matter of her Kingdom's safety. She brushed aside her pride for a moment, even though it stabbed her from the inside.

"I apologise, apologise for the way I talked to you in court that day in front of everyone. If you want to punish someone then punish me, don't punish the King or the innocent citizens of this Kingdom. They had no hand in it whatsoever".

Cameron looked thoughtful for a while, a wicked grin spread across his face, his canines glinting dangerously at the corner of his lips, " No I'm not withdrawing it. Darling, consider this my way of punishing you."

AUTHORS NOTE

Hey guys, I know it has been a long time since I posted but I got caught up with my exams and updating my other new book but since it's the holidays now I'm going to try to update it regularly. But btw, how have ur holidays been and how was the new chap?

Real question is how many of you want to punch Cameron in the face?

Vote! Comment and Share! And add this book to your libraries for notifications whenever I update. Also if any of u wants to make memes for this book then u can DM me and I'll add it in my next chapters.

ix. Looking for Angels

Sagarika furiously threw a rock into the temple pond.

'No I don't accept it'

She picked up another stone and flung it. Her muscles ticked each time she heard his voice, she had to keep her pride aside to apologise to him and he took the opportunity to break it. It almost seemed as if he had the upper hand.

It was almost afternoon and she had to be in her palace before lunch but she didn't feel like going back. She knew that Sulekha must be handling her absence but her brother was a person hard to convince. Neelsingh was more like his mother, too observant and nagging for his own good, it was time that they bound to knew her disappearance and Sulekha wasn't exactly an exceptional liar.

As she turned back to leave, she accidentally bumped into someone. "S-Sorry, my bad", she said dazedly.

"Wait", the person called out. Sagarika looked up saw their face, it was a British women. Sagarika internally groaned, she was done with their type of people.

"Are you Princess Saga- reeka"? The woman asked, mispronouncing her name.

"Sagarika. Yes I am, why"? Sagarika pronounced correctly, observing her suspiciously.

"Oh yes. Sagarika. I'm Lydia Hendricks, we met at the Ball earlier, you asked me the time, remember"? The woman, Lydia, introduced herself, making an attempt on pronouncing the name properly. Sagarika remained silent for a moment before recalling the first time when she met Lydia as the European women whom she asked for the time.

"Um...yes I suppose so.....How are you"? Sagarika asked awkwardly, not knowing what to reply back.

Luckily for her, Lydia smiled genuinely, "I'm fine. I just wanted to ask, did you knew someone by the name Esther Woods"?

"Yes, yes I did. Esther was my friend", Sagarika nodded frantically.

"Shall we take a seat here by the steps. It won't long enough, I just want to talk something really important to you", Lydia beseeched. Sagarika hesitated for a while, she wanted to go back to the Palace but here was seemingly nice woman wanting to talk to her. She couldn't say no. Sagarika nodded and sat down.

Lydia followed her and took a seat, smoothing out her layers of petticoat. Seeing her Sagarika felt bad, at least her skirt wasn't so puffed out and heavy. It was of a rather silky texture and loose, in contrast to the heavy yet thin Rajasthani Lehengas.

"So um... about Esther, how long have you known her"? Lydia asked.

"For about a seven months till now. Why is there a problem"?

Lydia pursed her lips, "Actually yes. Esther has moved back to London two weeks ago. She got married".

"What", Sagarika whispered in a stupor. She couldn't process what Lydia told a couple minutes ago. Then she looked back to times when letter sent to Esther would always remained unanswered.

"Yes, she did. She got married to the Viscount Glissbell, their marriage was decided nearly three months ago. I'm guessing she didn't tell you"? Lydia asked as she explained.

"No, no she did not! But if it was decided three months ago then why didn't she inform me of it"? Sagarika exclaimed as she finally realised the reason to the unanswered letters that she sent Esther since the last two weeks.

"Esther did not want to marry. Being married to a Viscount is not all glam and glitter as it sounds, the job is tough. And once you're the new Viscountess, your every single move would be judged and scrutinised." Sagarika could relate to that. She knew the hierarchies of European peerages, it wasn't very different from a royal one. The tutor hired by her father was a learned one whom had went abroad for higher education. It was the least he could do for Sagarika when she was supposed to be confined among the Fort walls for seventeen years.

Lydia continued, "Esther was sure that she could break the marriage. She loved India and wanted to adapt to the culture here.....she even wanted to get married to a local and run off to the hills of Shimla but luck wasn't on her side. Her parents were not aware of her interior plans, all they knew was that they didn't want Esther to become a spinster all her life, so they boarded her to the next ship to England. It was all so sudden, Esther was not aware of it and that's why she could not inform you of her departure".

Everything slowly got itself absorbed into Sagarika's mind. She felt bad for Esther and for herself. Besides Sulekha, The Woods girl was the only friend she had and now she was gone in a blink of an eye. Those seven months almost seemed like minutes to her. They passed on too quickly and were nothing more than just past memories.

Sagarika wondered what would happen to herself when Esther, who didn't like the idea of marriage, got forced by her parents and shipped off to another country. She shuddered to think that her own parents would do something like that. But then again she was a princess and being a princess people could use her for only one thing. A political pawn for her kingdom.

Lucky ones forged their own destiny but those fortunate ones were scarce. She considered her friend Laxmibai for instance. The girl was married of at fourteen despite being given lessons in fighting. She knew that her parents wanted her to marry the prince of Mihir for political purposes and nothing more, then the family of Mihir would expect her to produce heirs for the kingdom. That was what her entire life meant.

She knew that Esther too has faced a particular situation. Being pushed into a family of nobility for political reasons. She wondered if she could see her again or the last time they met at the ball was their farewell.

"I don't understand, why are you telling me all this"? Sagarika asked, facing Lydia.

"Because Esther is my cousin," Lydia stated, making Sagarika's eyes go wide and her mouth do drop.

"And she told me to tell you this as her egress was quite abrupt, she also told me to give you this letter," The Hendricks girl proceeded, her nimble hands reaching out a clean envelope.

Sagarika gingerly took it in her hands and unfolded it.

Dear Sagarika,

As you read this letter, I would probably be gone. You might be thinking about what this stupid girl is muttering about but I will convey everything to you neatly.

I am getting married. I should have told this to you earlier but my prideful head has constricted me from doing so as I lived in a fantasy that I might be able to break off this wedding. Clearly it has not happened as I'm currently writing to you from a ship that will leave for London in a matter of short time.

I wish we had more time. These seven months were not enough and the past two years were not enough for experiencing the entirety of a India. Unlike the others who came here of dreaming to conquer it, I wanted to live it. I wanted to make my dream of going to Shimla a reality but I suppose it will remain a broken dream forever.

Sagarika, don't worry about India. I have a feeling that Colonial rule would not last for long in this country. It's too strong and influential for that, call me seer or a person who's giving unwanted condolences but I feel like it's my intuition.

Dear Sagarika, stay strong in these upcoming years of your life. If you want something then fight for it. Fight for it until your last breath if you're passionate about it, do not let the opinions or logic of others sway you from your path. Be an olive tree in a storm.

My cousin Lydia is there to remind you of me. Befriend her, she's a nice lass. You would never be alone. I hope we see each other once more in better conditions.

Sagarika closed the letter and turned towards Lydia, "Thank you."

Lydia waved her hand dismissively, "It's alright, but I need you to give me something in place of the thanks. Can we be friends"? She asked, lighting up like a toddler who received a candy.

Sagarika chuckled, she noticed the difference between Esther and her cousin. Lydia was definitely younger than her sister and had strawberry blonde hair in contrast to Esther's honey coloured hair but the only thing common between the both cousins were their blue eyes.

"Why not? I feel bad about not being able to see Esther anymore but...."

"Don't worry about that, I'm Esther's cousin and people say that I could pass off as her twin if not for the hair", Lydia chimed, indicating towards her red locks. "Also, Esther used to tell me lot about you but I never got the chance to meet you until the Ball, but even there I lost the opportunity to introduce myself properly".

Sagarika smiled, "Well I'm glad to have formally met you".

Sagarika and Sulekha ran about the palace corridors, the latter trying to remain dignified as she did so. The court hearings were about start soon and they were already late. They slowed down their pace as they entered the balcony reserved for them, covered in a netted cloth.

Surprisingly, Cameron was an attendee too, seated in a regal chair mostly reserved for the ministers, but then again he was no less then one. In fact, Sagarika felt that in true sense the King and his ministers were just puppets whose strings were pulled by him. Despite being way younger than the king and other officials of the court, he knew how to make the king dance to his tunes. Begrudgingly she had to admit it, even though he was just twenty one summers old, he was well versed in politics and had a knack to sway his elders.

Most of the court hearings were quite mundane and so was this. Her father, Aditya and her mother, Shantidevi were seated together in a vast golden throne. Her mother wasn't allowed to directly involve in political affairs unless it was much needed. The hearings went smoothly with Cameron throwing her occasional glances that were met by scornful frown from Sagarika, replied by smug smirks.

Cameron cleared his throat, drawing the attention of others.

"Yes Captain Lowell, would you like to convey something"? The King asked in fake politeness as he felt his nerves twist underneath his skin when he saw a grave look in his hazel eyes.

"Definitely ,your highness. I would like to make a declaration", he paused, looking around the fear stricken faces of some of the courtiers and the Royal couple themselves. "Let the prices on the troops be reduced to the original amount as they were before I assumed my position."

Every single soul present at the court, including that of the maids and soldiers, were flabbergasted. They did not expect such a proclamation, and that too from the likes of a man such as Cameron.

Aditya almost chocked, he turned to face his wife. Shantidevi seemed equally stunned as him, but she had covered it better than her King. Neelsingh, who was mostly present at every court hearing as his duty as the Crown Prince and the Future king of Rangarh, seemed to inherit his mother's regality. If he was shocked as the others, he didn't show it.

Cameron felt smug internally as he saw Sagarika's dumbfounded features from the corner of his eye. She looked as still as a statue beside her lady - in - waiting whom he had seen many a times but never bothered to remember her name. He subtly smirked in her direction, bringing her estranged soul back to her body.

When she heard Cameron's proclamation, Sagarika's mouth flew open and her hands went still by her side from fiddling with the hem of her uttariya.

Aditya sputtered when, "Well, in that case, I must thank you....so be it.. ...Deepender," He called out, facing his Financial minister, "Make an announcement in the kingdom that the taxes would be back to their original values, and return the recent taxes back to their respectful payers."

Deepender nodded and made a note in his scroll.

Shantidevi smiled, her smile fixed and strained, "Whatever the reason be, we're grateful for it. Aren't we, Son"? She implored, looking back at Neelsingh with a forced smile.

Neelsingh narrowed his eyes at the statement, "Yes, yes, why shouldn't we"? He agreed absentmindedly, as a train of thoughts ran his head. If there was one quality that can't be neglected under any circumstances would definitely be his overtly suspicious and paranoid behaviour.

For a split second his eyes traveled to the balcony before returning back to stare the Resident in the eye. Sulekha was the only one who had the presence of mind to meet his. Her lips were set in a straight line. The only one who was not pleased with the entire state of affairs was Sebastian. His hands were clenched at his sides as his jaw ticked.

"Sire! This is an unacceptable excuse! You and I bloody well know that you have no care for these brown peasant rubbish! Why would you do something scandalous as such"? The latter spat out bitterly as he and Cameron were walking out of the Court along the royal garden trails.

Cameron stopped and faced him, narrowing his eyes, "Do not question me Sebastian, it might not do you any good besides I have a—"

Before he could complete his sentence, he saw Sagarika running towards him with her hands clutching her purple skirt, slightly lifting it above the ground.

She came to a halt and stood in a proper composure, "I hope I didn't intrude on anything important?" Cameron shook his head while Sebastian remained rigid than ever.

"You did not", he replied.

Sagarika smiled nervously as she fiddled subconsciously with her stole, "I did not expect whatever that happened on the court earlier because of today morning but.....thank you. What ever on earth made you change your mind, I'm glad for that." She rambled, not knowing how to bear the intimidating aura of the two men in front of her.

Cameron shrugged, "Well I did think about what you said earlier and when I saw that the Princess herself got her hands dirty in these matters....I was moved, honestly. I'm not the Devil that you assume me to be, Princess".

Sagarika didn't know what to reply but she did feel the intense gaze of Sebastian boring holes in her face. She didn't mind him, instead she gave a stiff smile to Cameron and left before saying.

"I'm grateful for it".

Sebastian turned sourly towards Cameron, "So, this is your reason"? He sneered, gesturing at Sagarika's retreating form. "What will you answer to the Company about the sudden decrease in the prices, may I ask?

"Trust me Sergeant, I am well aware about my actions and the answer to Company's queries is my personal problem. You need not worry about it, by the way I am in a dire need of mulled wine. It's really cold here", Cameron replied casually, rubbing his shoulders in an attempt to warm himself when Rangarh's biting cold winds whooshed past him, bringing colour to his pale face.

But unknown to the two of them, someone was observing their impromptu meeting from afar.....someone, who watched them earlier when Sagarika and Cameron first met in the rose gardens.

And none of them felt the lingering gaze of the intruder, boring holes into their bodies.

x. Glass Minds

G auri had officially proclaimed Raina to be possessed.

Ever since Raina had that vision attack from their visit to the Residency, Gauri was convinced that Sagarika's ghost had possessed Raina. The latter rebuked her accusations but Gauri was sure of it.

"Maybe Sagarika wants to tell you the truth of her story but since she's already dead, she's trying to get it through you. I think that's why you're getting those crazy visions of her and that British guy".

That was her firm answer to it. Raina wanted to admit her theory but what held her back was the inability to feel Sagarika, if her ghost was really creating those hallucinations in the back of her mind, almost made her dismiss the theory.

She never shared this information with anyone except Gauri. Not even her parents, she didn't want to share such a sensitive information as this with them. The odds of them taking it casually was as less as her having her privacy respected.

Even her Grandmother did not earn her trust despite being the only family member she was close with.

The visions were creepy and not easy to understand but having Cameron's diary made it easier to understand only an aspect of the situation since it was from the late Resident's point of view and not Sagarika's.

Worst part yet was that after ten minutes of coming back to reality, she could only remember bits and pieces of it, it almost felt like a shock therapy but without the anaesthesia.

She ran through the entires in the journal, in search of an answer to her previous vision. There it was, inscribed in a yellowed page the date marked with faded ink as 24 November 1848. Apparently Cameron had mixed feelings about the way the meeting went with Sagarika that day. He felt conflicted when both personal and professional matters intersected at the wrong time.

She approached me but I have lacked the courage to help her. Instead, I had hurt her with harsh words and insulted her apology.

But what can I do? How will I be able to help her when I myself am stuck in a condition that would attract the questions of all senior officials? I knew it was a horrible decision to develop a heart for the Princess. What was I thinking? She's the enemy, a person far from my reach.

Of course there are European women better than her in England. Alas, a women who has fire and a sense of independence is hard to find.I can't seem to get her out of my head, why does she invade my senses? Coming to India was a despicable idea.

I feel the worst. I hate myself to the core.

Raina felt bad. Even though she detested the idea of her beloved town being under the hands of a wannabe tyrant dictator, she tried to look in a another view. People tend to forget that Cameron was only 21 at that time.

Just a year older than Raina.

If he belonged to the 21st century, then at that age, he would rather be focused on surviving his senior year in College than being a pawn of the Company.

Honestly, when she thought about it deeply, she realised that Sagarika and Cameron grew up too quickly for their young age and were thrust into the world where it was either kill or be killed.

She found it much easier to understand Cameron's actions when she kept her patriotic emotions asides and look from a humanist perspective. He wore a mask, a mask that confidently said that he had everything under control in stark contrast to reality.

He wasn't bad but wasn't good either.

She wanted to know more about the two pairs but did not get enough time or information. The least she could do was wait for the visions to come roaring back because Cameron's entires wasn't enough to under-stand everything.

Time did not seem to be on her side, her mother stopped her yesterday and threw a bomb, informing her that they were going to leave for Delhi tomorrow morning. Raina internally slapped her forehead.

Of course, how could she forget about it! They had scheduled to meet Aarush and his family in Delhi. She nearly lost memory of it due to a hundred and seventy years affair.

She threw in a bundle of clothes in a blue suitcase as she thought about the messed up scenario.

Gladly they were only going away for two days. Raina still had a month left before her summer break ends and before that she was determined to crack the case of Rangarh's last princess.

The last time she had ever been to Delhi was during a two-week school trip. Raina was upset that Gauri couldn't make it to the school trip but she went in spite of her absence, sole reason she loved to travel. Luckily, she wasn't alone, Keshav went along.

Though she was never close friends with him, he was a good friend since Raina was the only bridge between him and his crush on Gauri. Thinking about Keshav made her revisit the time she met him after a long time. Did his crush on Gauri survive or has it been dissolved over time? It certainly did not seem to go away given the fact that he was grinning the same way he did in senior year of High school.

She did not have time to think about her friend's crush when other pressing matters were on hands. Raina said her temporary goodbyes to her other family members staying back. Her grandmother pulled her into a hug before she left , but what took Raina back was the sudden whisper of warning, "Some people are like the moon. They show only half of their pretty face but their dark side are revealed only on occasion."

Raina pulled back from the hug with a scandalous face, her smiled strained as she moved away from the old woman who looked rather unfazed. It seemed like she knew something that Raina did not even have a clue about.

When she got into the cab, Sheela came near her window and rolled her eyes, whispering sharply, "Don't mind her. She's getting old".

Raina's eyes widened at it. She respected and loved her grandma lot, and she expected Sheela to do the same but was aghast at her unexpected words.

She shook her head and silently scolded her not to say so. Sheela grinned back at her.

Raina haven't left Rangarh much, well except for College, but it had been years since she had ever set foot on an airport. They had to travel all the way to Gwalior in Madhya Pradesh for the nearest Airport since Rangarh was near the borders of Madhya Pradesh.

She loved flights, even though they were tiring at times but this one was a short one of almost one and a half an hour. She instantly occupied the window one. Raina admitted it, she was quite childish at times.

Delhi was hot this time of the year. And by hot, it was burning a forty five degrees out there. "Where do they live? The Mehras I mean"? Raina asked as they got into a taxi and urged the driver to switch on the air conditioning for starters.

"Jor Bagh", Her mother answered.

'Ah why not' To be honest, Raina wasn't the least bit surprised. She expected a posh locality for their Residence. She had definitely heard about Jor Bagh. It was an expensive area on South East Delhi being the home to many ministers and upscale people. Not to mention the famous Khan Market and Lodhi Gardens.

The Mehras definitely had an upgraded house for starters. It was a Bungalow with a huge glass window that displayed a crystal chandelier hung from the ceiling with yellow lights illuminating the interiors. The neighbourhood was calm and quiet with only the chirruping of birds echoing in the distance.

Raina felt nervous. This was the second time they were meeting the Mehra family and their CEO of a son. She still remembered his whiskey coloured eyes that pierced right through her body. Although they weren't that impactful as Cameron's.

'Ugh, snap of it, Raina' She mentally grumbled, shaking her head subtly. Mr and Mrs Mehras were the ones to greet them inside their house and good news was that Aarush was still in his office. Bad news? He was gonna be back soon.

After having lunch together, Lakshmi Mehra showed her and her mother around her house while Roop and Mr. Mehra wandered in about their business in the terrace. Raina was admiring a mural of Lord Buddha on the first floor. It was detailed quite well, hued grey and blue with engravings of golden marigolds.

"Hello". Raina gasped and nearly jumped in fright. She turned back, holding her chest and wanted to give a piece of her mind to the person who so abruptly disturbed her, when she realised who it was.

Aarush.

"Um..hi. You almost scared me", Raina chuckled nervously while she stammered. Aarush wasn't in the least concerned, his gaze travelled to the mural on the wall.

"I see that you like it".

"I find it beautiful", Raina answered uncertainly.

"I made that".

"Oh", Raina was taken aback. "I didn't know you were into art".

"I was. I made that during the holidays after my boards. I had nothing to do so this idea struck and I gave it life by clay and oil paints. I can't see why my parents still insist on having it here".

"I don't see why not. I mean it looks nice".

Aarush hummed in response as he glided a finger through the golden marigolds. " When did you arrive, Raina", the way her name rolled off his tongue smoothly without hesitation or shyness, it sent a shiver down her spine.

"A-An hour ago I guess", She stuttered, mentally slapping herself for being nervous around him. She wished she was more confident like the other girls at College, Raina hated herself for being meek whenever conversing with the opposite sex.

"How long does it take for you to reach home and..office"? She asked in an attempt to break the awkward silence between them.

Aarush did not meet her eyes. " forty three minutes", he replied curtly.

"Why didn't you move to Gurgaon personally? I mean, I feel those forty three minutes to be quite long and staying nearby would be convenient for moving to and from your office", Raina asked, curious as to why he had to stay far away from his workplace. The travel from here and there can be tiring after a long day of work, especially when you had to head an entire company from executives to interns.

Aarush snapped his head back to her direction. His eyes stayed fixed over her face, that was when he noticed the way her umber hair was closed into braid that rested upon her shoulder, reaching well past her midriff. Her forehead was covered by a strand of hair styled into a sideswept bang.

This was the second time he noticed her. First being the time in Rangarh, her form draped in that beautiful lavender saree and her hair left free instead of being in the tight braid it was. Aarush hated to admit it but he was definitely smitten by the town girl near him. Never in his life had romance been the first thing on his mind, certainly not when he had his ambitions checked.

He was wealthy. Even since the time of his Pre school days, he was privileged having everything at his beck and call. There was never a moment where girls would not stop giggling or staring at him throughout High school or College. Yet he never did so as to glance their way either.

Aarush knew the vain wishes of his parents. To get him married to a girl of their choice. He was reluctant when his parents announced the news of a possible bride but he went along, just to fulfil their demands as a debt for inheriting the software company he was so passionate about. However, everything changed when his eyes met Raina.

He was ready to agree to a futile marriage just for their sake and then ignore the presence of his future wife for the entirety of his life.

But for Raina, no.

All the cold walls that he built around him came crashing. There was something familiar and alluring about the girl he met. And he was determined to keep her unlike the others.

No, he wanted her.

"Um..well, I have been thinking about moving somewhere near but I'm not sure. Maybe after marriage or so. You don't have to worry about my travels, I have a driver to escort me anywhere I want", He answered abruptly. Raina felt disheartened, she wanted Aarush to open himself more but it seemed that the more she tried the more he pushed her out.

How was she supposed to work this alliance if one was so reluctant to cooperate? She finally came to a conclusion that Aarush Mehra was not an easy person to talk to.

Raina sighed and turned to leave. She felt awkward being in the presence of someone so stiff, so the least she could do is stick by her mother and Mrs. Mehra's side.

"Wait"! The familiar voice of Aarush called out. This time, a little to raised. Raina turned around from the staircase. She could see that Aarush was hesitant about something but nevertheless patiently waited for him to say something.

Aarush ran his fingers over his dark hair and licked off the dryness of his lips. He let out a deep breath when he saw the raised eyebrow of Raina looking expectantly at him.

"Can we um....are you available this evening? I can show you around Jor Bagh and we can go out to Khan Market if you like", Aarush volunteered, his eyes being genuinely considerate for the first time since they ever met.

"I heard from your mother that you like books and Khan Market is famous for its bookshops. What do you say"? He prodded further with a smile gracing his face.

Raina was baffled. Seeing a smile on his face was as rare as having her room locked without being disturbed. But how could she refuse when the person she thought to be difficult was finally taking a step? Besides, she knew how her mother would love it if she spends a day out with him.

He asked and she said yes.

"Sure, why not"?

xi. Is it true?

R aina was agitated and confused.

She kept prancing about the lengths of her hotel room, she was glad about the fact that her parents were willing to buy an extra room just for herself, but of course, it meant that they had the full rights to barge in any moment provided.

She kept muttering furiously under her breath as the call for Gauri kept ringing on. "C'mon, c'mon, just pick the goddamn phone, Gau"!

After what seemed like ages, Gauri finally picked up the call at the last ring, "Hey, sorry I was in the shower. What's the matter? How's everything going"?

"Took you long enough! And to your question, NO! Everything is so messed up right now", Raina was impatient with her tone. She immediately started filling Gauri in with every single detail about her so - called date with Aarush.

The more she spoke about it, the more she got anxious, and the more she got anxious the more Gauri grew confused about the entire ordeal.

"You sure it was him? Like his face and demeanour....did it all match"? She asked frantically, trying to pry more hidden information from Raina.

"Yes!" The latter exclaimed. "It was through and through him, Gau! His face and eyes, it was all him I swear"!

"Okay, okay, calm down. Are you sure that's what it showed you"?

"Yes, Gauri. That's what I've been saying the past ten minutes"! Raina fretted. She ran a hand through her dark locks and collapsed on the soft mattress with the phone still pressed against her ear.

Her outing with Aarush was a lot disturbing than she expected it to be. It was definitely one of the most confused and hopeless moment of her life. It had nothing to do with Aarush....well, atleast nothing indirectly.

Suffice to say, Raina received another wave of Sagarika's vision, right when Aarush dropped her off at the hotel lobby. She immediately sprinted up to her room after giving cautious mumbles to her overbearing mother.

"Hold still, princess", Sulekha scolded as she wrapped the uttariya around Sagarika's arms in an elaborate style. Sagarika's jade-stained irises stared upon her reflection on the mirror, narrowing as the material prickled her skin.

"Is it odd that I find the Sengars to be interested in the affairs of a kingdom that holds ties with the British? It's not likely of them to do so, they find kingdoms in liege with the firangis to be traitors. I wonder what mother and father are planning", Sagarika mused, bringing about the attention of Sulekha who so as subtly glanced at the former's reflection.

"Whatever it be, I hope it does not bring trouble to the kingdom," She commented, adjusting the folds of Sagarika's skirt. It was a busy day , not only for Sulekha as it was usually, but for the entire Vermas.

After all it was the day Crown Prince Ishir Sengar of Mihir was arriving.

Sagarika held a look of annoyance ever since morning, wether it was while bathing or having breakfast, the grumpy look never left her face much to Shantidevi's disappointment.

"Do try to put up an act of niceties in front of him, he is after all your fiancé"! She scolded her sharply as they waited outside the balcony overlooking upon the kingdom for the procession of the Prince's entourage. Sagarika merely huffed at her words, the miffed look not yet leaving her gentle feminine features.

When the arrival of the Sengar Prince was announced, Sagarika and the other royal ladies were rushed to the drawing room of the palace. It was decorated more extravagantly than usual with respect to the accommodation of the Prince of Mihir.

That's when she saw him.

Yuvraj Ishir Sengar of Mihir.

And to Raina's horror, the exact replica of Aarush Mehra.

Raina tried to forget the horrible coincidental image but it was not that easy when your fiancé looked exactly like some dead prince of another kingdom from centuries ago.

She couldn't wrap her head after that because whatever happened after catching a glimpse of his appearance was a blur. She thought it was maybe because of the shock of seeing the eerie resemblance between Ishir and Aarush that weighed out the other memories.

Right now she felt overwhelmed. She cursed her luck. Raina had a history of overthinking about usual stuff but this? Nah, her mind wasn't going to leave her alone without forming a series of unnatural scenarios that she can't escape from.

She tried reliving the memories again and again, hoping to find a loophole that would prove that it was merely her mind playing tricks on her and Prince Ishir did not look like Aarush. But things weren't that easy, Ishir and Aarush did look similar and no matter the amounts of denials Raina had, there was no refusing it.

Her brain clearly showed her. He definitely looked like Aarush but with a change in clothing and age. She saw him, decked in fine coloured silks and a golden circlet that enclosed around his forehead with intricate designs. Ishir looked rather young than Aarush, she remembered how Queen Shantidevi described his age to be that of nineteen.

But the real question was.....

How?

How can two entirely different people look the same?

Of course she had heard the theory of doppelgängers, two non-related people looking similar but, doppelgängers can't look exactly. There was difference between similar and exact.

Gauri's voice from the other side pulled her back into the present, "Raina, what if.... Ishir and Aarush are the same people? I mean, what if Ishir reincarnated as Aarush? Chances are high you know...I mean....look at the way Ishir was introduced to Sagarika and the way Aarush was introduced to you? They all were quite the same, a marriage alliance! Just think about it".

Raina raised her eyebrows in a judgmental way. "Are you fucking serious?—", Raina coughed as she realised that she used a swear word and continued, "Next you'll be harping that I'm Sagarika, isn't it"?

"Now that you've mentioned it, I'm actually seeing the picture. What if you're not possessed by Sagarika, but you're Sagarika herself? Think about it, you're only getting visions from Sagarika's perspective and especially when you're at places or situations that are somehow connected to her. Doesn't this all make a connection of some sort"?

Raina closed her eyes and rubbed her temples. She knew that her friend was the most rational one of the two but her baseless accusations created an otherwise doubt in Raina's head. Clearly the entire deal of Sagarika was messing up with both their heads, first possession and now incarnation? Gauri needed help.

She immediately disconnected the call and went to her suitcase. Along with her other necessities, she brought Cameron's diary in case another vision erupted during her stay in Delhi. And true to her intuitions, it did come.

The entries in his diary gave her to clues of Ishir's life. Being the prince of Mihir, he hated the East India Company to the core than any other royalties of that time and well, the feeling was mutual, except the Governer - General of India during that time, Dalhousie, was greatly distrustful of the Sengars. To be honest, it seemed like the entirety of India's royalties found the Sengars to be a mysterious lot who never associated directly with other royal clans.

By the looks of Cameron's entries, he seemed to loathe him. Understand-able, she thought, in view of the infamous affair between him and Sagarika. His entries told that according to rumours at that era, Ishir and his family used to engage in illegal affairs and even dabbled in the dark arts, something that Raina scoffed at. There were more crazier allegations about the family of Mihir, in one of his descriptions, he stated that they captured a group of girls to whom they would feed poison from a young age until a few survive into women hood, their veins filled with various concoction of deadly poison.

Vishkanyas, as the locals termed.

A band of femme fatales who had the ability to destroy kingdoms and cities with sexual contact or a mere kiss. A theory that Raina closely associated with poison ivy. Cameron mentioned how these practices were used back in ancient India during the time of Chandragupta Maurya and has been discarded ever since.

But the Sengars never admitted nor appreciated such assumptions. They denied being involved in such affairs, however, others were never convinced.

So naturally when the Company got to know that the Vermas had violated the subsidiary alliance, they got mad, but more so at the fact that they violated it for the Sengars. Cameron wrote how it boiled his blood when the principal aim for their violation was the marriage proposal for Sagarika.

The means by which the Company got the knowledge about it seemed quite selfish and confusing to her.

A letter was sent to Cameron by Sagarika.

xii. Even When It Hurts

An antique vanity table glared back at Raina as she stood outside the bedroom of Sagarika inside the Rangarh fort. Her chamber was locked permanently by glass. She wondered if the place remained untouched as it was 64 years ago, there was no specific name plate that mentioned it to be Sagarika's room but she knew it, she knew it from the memories of Sagarika where she used to spend most of her years.

But the chamber wasn't the exact as it portrays itself to onlookers. Raina still has the vivid memories of the late Princess's room, there were many things missing from the room, probably due to time such as the big mirror in which Sagarika used to gaze herself at and of course a life size painting of the said person.

Raina had a good idea of who might be behind the disappearance of the painting.

It had been two weeks ever since she returned to Rangarh from Delhi. And most importantly, two weeks ever since the ghastly vision of Aarush's doppelgänger.

After that incident, his presence near her made her more awkward than usual. She refused to meet his eyes in hopes that she won't have to recall

Ishir's face. When he bid her farewell in the airport, Raina's lips curled into a stiff smile and hurriedly rushed into the terminal without a word. That gesture made both the Mehras and the Yadavs to knit their eyebrows.

"Did I do something wrong", She could still hear his voice, laced with confusion, implore her through her phone.

She shook her head in response. "It's not like that", she mumbled absent-minded.

The last vision she received after that crazy one was on the way to Gwalior. She got a vision, or memory as Gauri liked to call it, mid flight. Luckily, she was zoned out before hand in order for her mother to notice anything out of the blue.

"My Lady, do not do this, I plead you. If the King gets knowledge of such a scandal then....god forbid to ever think of the consequences !"

Sulekha wailed as she tried to stop Sagarika from opening her vanity drawer by grabbing her wrists quite roughly and shoving her aside from the teak wood furniture. However, Sagarika wasn't the one to easily give up.

She shoved the former more violently until Sulekha almost hit her head upon the bed pillar.

"I'm advising you against this, Sagarika. Consequences shall be severe if you do so, this will call war"! Sulekha admonished as she steadied herself, helplessly watching Sagarika dip a pen in a pot of ink and scribble furiously on the paper set in front of her.

Sagarika paused and snapped her head so quick that it would have broke her delicate neck, but she was too livid to even care about her well being. Her green eyes pierced right through Sulekha's dark ones.

"No one shall know about this unless we tell them ourselves, so do me a favour and keep your lips sealed for heaven's sake"!

"What's the assurance that he will keep his lips sealed"? Sulekha taunted, scoffing derisively at her mistress's belief.

"He will. He has to for the sake of his duty. I trust him on this more than I do you", The Verma Princess replied snidely, having the least bit of care for Sulekha's feelings as they shook upon the weight of her shrewd words.

"Oh is that so"?

"Unfortunately yes. Because you seem so keen on siding with the others to even care about my life or for that sake my feelings! Ever since I was born I have been tied under the anchors of traditions and practice of this family! No one has the right to decide my life, not you, not my parents and not anyone. And you ought to know this better than anyone else in this damned Kingdom"!

Sagarika's reddened lips curled into a spiteful smirk as she provoked her, " Oh, I understand now. You're the one who's eager to get married aren't you? Isn't that what you want, Sulekha? To get a nice husband and slave away your short life for him like a good wife"?

"If that's what you desire, then who am I to bound you in shackles of royal duties? Speak Sulekha and I shall relieve you of your position in this palace".

Sulekha blinked back the tears that formed a thin sheet around her eyes. She wasn't the one to cry, not even when her father was shot in front of her eyes, or when her mother was on her deathbed, suffering from leprosy. But now the words of her friend, a sister whom she considered her to be, stung her from deep within.

Yes, it was true that once a princess was married off, the lady - in- waiting would be found a suitable groom from one of the nobilities for their service to the royal family. But that wasn't the case! She could see that Sagarika was misunderstanding her concern for her own selfish needs. She was just worried about the wrath of the Sengars and it didn't help the fact that they weren't exactly the good lot of people.

"You have misunderstood my words. I never intended to get married. If that's what you feel , then.." Sulekha stepped forward and looked at Sagarika directly, "I'll personally help you deliver this god forbidden letter".

Sagarika's lips parted in surprise as her perfectly arched eyebrows turned up, "You will?"

Sulekha nodded firmly, "I will".

Sagarika stared at the lotus pond, fiddling with a pale pink petal as Cameron's jaws tightened and his pale hands clenched around an open letter, popping his veins out prominently in the golden sunlight. He glared indirectly at the royal Princess, his eyes narrowing to slits.

"What were they thinking? Does the King really thinks highly of himself"? He seethed as muted anger rose around his senses.

Sagarika rolled her eyes, her olive fingers that gently tugged on the petal now harshly tore it away from the flower. She tossed it aside and said, " Well, to be honest, they were definitely trying to defy the Company by using me as the spawn for their dirty games." She sighed and continued dramatically after seeing the absolute look of rage in his eyes, " By having Mihir on their side they can definitely withstand any future attacks from your men".

Cameron arched one his brow and chuckled dryly , "Oh, is that what that old fool is planning?"

Sagarika shrugged nonchalantly.

He analysed her for a minute. There was something off about her behaviour. "And even if he did, why should I trust you, princess? Aren't you the one to hate us for trying to enslave your land, wouldn't you benefit from this alliance, after all, isn't that what you want? The have the upper hand?

That threw her off the track.

"Maybe, but not like this. A stupid marriage isn't what I will ever have in mind. Do you have anything else to say or are we gonna do something about it"? Sagarika deadpanned as she inspected her nails. Her eyes challenging him.

God how he hated and loved those eyes.

Those very same eyes that challenged him the first time they met. He was never going to forget those bold, kohl lined ones even when he while suffering in Hell.

He snapped back to reality and snarled at her words, throwing his hands up infuriated. "God ! Are you always this snappy"?

Sagarika arched an eyebrow, "I've always been this snappy.....just a lot around you for some reason".

She didn't hear the string of colourful words that escaped his mouth, but she did hear him mutter something vaguely under his breath, "Insolent brat"!

"Excuse me"?

He whipped around with his eyes flashing dangerously, "Do you desire my help or not"?

"Of course I do".

"Then I suggest you stop being so disrespectful towards me and start acknowledging my position! I'm not someone who you can puppet around. Not especially when you're in such a state".

"You will help me no matter what, wether you like it or not, because we both know how much of a threat the Company considers Mihir to be, so you don't really have a choice", Sagarika replied haughtily, glad that the one in a fix was the Captain and not her.

Cameron remained still for a while before bursting into laughter. It wasn't one of amusement , but reminded her of the same mock tone from their last meeting ever. His laughs soon slowed into dark chuckles.

"I don't face a choice? Darling, you're seriously mistaken for. Yes, it's true that we consider the Sengars as a threat but that doesn't mean we have other ways to.....discard them. For starters, we can always start a war against your kingdom or... make use of the Subsidiary Alliance in a different direction, OR....we can always kill you".....

Sagarika took a step back, stunned and appalled. She hoped she heard him wrong.

Or...we can always kill you

But she was sorely mistaken. He meant what he said as she watched him procure a silver knife from his coat pockets and fiddle lackadaisically with it. His eyes gleaming fanatically with sadism.

"What do you..." her voice trailed off before she can complete her sentence. She clutched her blood red skirt and subconsciously stepped back as she watched him move forward, the knife twirling lithely around his fingers.

"You", he swiped the knife, pointing its edge towards her, smirking wickedly as he continued, "have always been a weed in our plans, foiling it the moment you sniff it out like bloodhound. If we could get rid of you, Mihir will be taken out easily. It will be like two birds in a single shot".

"Poor Rangarh. Then they won't have anyone else to use for a safe alliance with Mihir. Lest the King has another daughter that is".

Her back hit a tree and her breath hitched in her throat as the proximity between them was just an hair breadth away.

"But he does not", His breath fanned her ears as he whispered callously in them. Her form shivered at the action, bringing him an oddly sickening sense of satisfaction.

She knew what he was accusing her off. Sagarika caught tiffs from people she hired to spy on the Cantonment and it's official members. Numerous times they have made plans to ruin Rangarh but each time they tried, they failed.

And Cameron knew exactly who was behind it all. Yet, he remained silent. For God knows what reason.

The cold tip of the knife reached underneath her chin, raising her head to face Cameron's gold flecked - hazel eyes. Her eyes widened at his next words.

"I can kill you and dispose your corpse off in this pond or bury it in the forest. Either way, no one would be able to find you."

xiii. Salted Wounds

Sagarika visible gulped at his words.

I can kill you and dispose your corpse off in this pond or bury it in the forest. Either way, no one would be able to find you.

The tip of his knife dug deeper, threatening to break her skin. Suddenly, Cameron's stiff lips twitched at the ends and the next thing she knew, he was laughing with mirth, his head thrown back and the knife left her chin.

She looked at him with confusion. Cameron stopped laughing, "My my, princess. You should have seen your face. It was more priceless than your entire jewellery".

The Verma princess now looked even more confused, and offended. She didn't know if his words were of jest or a means of flirting. Nope, it must have been the former.

Yet, she couldn't understand. Just a second ago he was threatening her with a knife and his eyes were filled with bitter rage, but now — he was...laug hing.

"Good Lord, you're dense", he taunted, smirking at her face as it immediately morphed from confusion to anger.

"Excuse me"? She stressed each word, resentment coating her voice.

"Do you actually believe that I would kill you? As much as tempting the idea seems, we have a witness. You're little henchwomen — err— whatever her name is, knows me to be the last person to ever see you and the mere mention of my presence can send your people spiralling."

Sagarika felt stupid. There was no lie in his words, she indeed was dense. If she had ever thought about the existence of Sulekha, she would've rebuffed his bluffs the second he whipped out that damned knife.

But if she had.....would she have felt his alluring closeness.

'Ugh, snap out of it' she mentally scolded herself before narrowing her eyes at him.

"That wasn't funny", her voice was sharp. Cameron raised a brow and titled his head, "Are you sure? Because I found the sight quite amusing. You're quite easy to pick on, you know?"

She groaned, rolling her eyes at him. There was no opportunity that this man could miss to humiliate her. She glanced at him again when a deep sigh left his lips. Surprisingly, a faint smile rested upon his lips rather than a mocking smirk. It made her wonder the thought that might be running in his mind, though she didn't had to for long.

"Allow me to cut straight to the chase, I will help you break of this alliance. No one deserves to be married off against their will — not even you", he said grimly, his gaze trained on the forest floor as he kicked a stray pebble into the pond.

She watched it skitter across the water before landing on a lotus pad, creating gentle ripples in the otherwise still water body. She knew what he was thinking about.

Esther

During her time spent with Esther, she gathered much information about Cameron, not will fully though. He and Esther used to be childhood friends since the young age of five. Esther's father was an officer the British Army and the another means of influence by which Cameron rose quickly to the ranks of a Resident. Sagarika recalled how Esther told her that there was a another member in their crew, David Hollers.

She vaguely remembered him to be the Resident of Jhansi from the accounts of her conversations with the Queen of Jhansi, Laxmibai.

She sympathised with him. Though he was a priggish being, Sagarika understood the pain of loosing a friend but she doubted it made much of a difference since he could come and go to England anytime he pleased. Unlike her.

"You're thinking about her aren't you, about Esther"?

That caught him off guard. He looked at her with faint surprise, "Did she tell you"?

Sagarika shook her head, "Lydia did".

She watched as realisation dawned upon his pale face, "I see that you have met her cousin. And to answer your question, yes, I was reminded of her. Though the both of you are to marry aristocrats, your desires oppose it, but I do bargain for some respect and acknowledgment taking in consideration that I am risking certain things for your demands. Do you have any idea on the amount of lies I had to utter in front of the Governer - General for the tax issues"?

"Not my fault. You're the one who increased them", She shrugged in a matter - of - factly manner.

Cameron scowled at her gesture. He felt his anger flare at her ignorance when he had to withstand the avalanche of intruding questions like a weed in the earth without giving any hint of his sinuous intentions , "Last time I knew, you came begging for it, and I took pity on you. And remember, this time I'm doing this for Esther...not for you".

Sagarika's brow quirked at it, "For Esther"? .

His gaze flicked to her, "Yes Sagarika, for Esther. Not everything is about you, your highness", he said as if her royal status left a bitter taste on his tongue, " You do realise that these favours aren't for free, right? You have to repay them".

Sagarika faltered, she knew making a deal with him was as good as selling her soul to the Devil, but unfortunately she had no choice, "And pray tell what might those be"?

"I shall inform you when the time for it arrives, until then keep that in mind," Cameron's voice cut off sharply, a clear indication of his annoyance of her.

Likewise, Sagarika too came off to be aggravated by Cameron's constant impropriety and hidden prejudice. She wasn't going to stand by let him belittle her like she was his personal servant. Heck, even a servant did not deserve to be treated as so.

"Fine, be that way"! Quiet immersed in a sea of rage, she failed to see a giant pebble in her way, her foot sole jigged on it absent mindedly causing her to slip , twisting her ankle in the impact.

"Argh", she let out a strangled cry as the hot pain from the injury seared through her leg. Being locked up in a palace since her birth and having the servants at your beck and call did not leave much room to come out of your comfort zone. And she hated it for that. She pressed upon the ankle joint only to regret it. More pain shot up at the response.

Hissing in pain, Sagarika tried to get up but the immobility of her leg prevented her from doing so. When her leg gave out in pain, an arm wrapped around her waist, swooping her up.

It was Cameron.

"Careful", he said and gently brought her near the edge of the pond. He lifted the red fabric of her skirt to inspect her foot. Beads of blood trickled as a result of her anklet piercing the skin, intensifying the pain to a slight burning sensation.

After struggling to remove the jewellery of her leg, he brought her feet in contact with the cold water of the pond. The dark green water soothed the pain but not shock that instilled inside of Sagarika.

She watched with wide eyes as Cameron took a seat near her and waited. His eyes downcast at a single lotus that swayed its petals in a lackadaisical manner. After what seemed like hours in silence, he lifted her foot to examine it, still swollen he put back into the water.

Though the cold pond water lapped away gently at her foot, easing the twisted pain slowly, it failed to extinguish the fiery rage burning in her heart. She sensed that there was something up with him, his fidgety behaviour, violent mood swings from one state to another, he wasn't the usual snarky Resident as he used to be before and it confused her. Sagarika felt as if he was hiding something from her, a secret that he wished not to share that seemingly must involve her in some or the other way, and it was the reason for her ire towards him . She stared at him unnervingly, her green eyes piercing like daggers that seemed to have no effect on Cameron . Her lips were set into a straight line.

"Is there something you would like to speak out. You seem to be having a confession", his voice and words added fuel to fire.

Straining herself to not raise her tone she spoke in a condescending way, "I have a confession, Captain? It looks like you're the one who seems to hide something. Better to let the tea spill, isn't it"? She crossed her arms and scrutinised him with narrowed eyes.

And try to her intuition, she saw him squirm uncomfortably on his seat with his eyes fidgeting anywhere but her. "I don't follow."

"You very well follow on what I'm talking about," She hissed.

"It's better if somethings are left buried", He snapped and stood up, leaving no room for the conversation to continue, " Go home and rest, try to move your leg gently once in a while. Not too much and do not add pressure to it. Good day, Princess".

"No wait ! Cameron, what do you know? What are you not telling me"? Sagarika yelled after him as he mounted his horse, but her words fell on deaf ears as he spared her a single glance and tugged on the reins, forcing the animal to take a sharp swerve and gallop away.